# THE LADY NEXT DOOR AND OTHER STORIES

---

## DARA GIRARD

# ALSO BY DARA GIRARD

## Collections

*Domestic Disturbance (written as Dara Benton)*

*Dark Love: Five Story Collection*

*Holiday Hearts*

*School Days: Five Story Collection*

*Lost and Found*

*Five Holiday Tales*

*10 Holiday Stories*

*When the Snow Falls*

## Henson Series

*Table for Two*

*Gaining Interest*

*Careless Rapture*

*Dangerous Curves*

*Familiar Stranger*

## Clifton Sisters

*The Sapphire Pendant*

*The Amber Stone*

*The Emerald Ring*

## Novels

*Honest Betrayal*

*The Daughters of Winston Barnett*

*Remember My Name*

*Illusive Flame*

*Winterwood Lane*

*Piece of Cake*

*This Changes Everything*

# CONTENTS


## THE LADY NEXT DOOR

The Lady Next Door     3

## A HOME FOR ADAM

A Home for Adam     23

## LOLA'S DECISION

Lola's Decision     43

## MISS LANA WILSON

Miss Lana Wilson     59

## A GIFT FOR PHILOMENA

A Gift for Philomena     79

*About the Author*     101

# THE LADY NEXT DOOR

# THE LADY NEXT DOOR

The dreadful woman was humming again. And loudly at that. She could hear her, even with her window shut. Mrs. Harmony Ellis looked out her kitchen window to see her new neighbor blissfully humming in her garden—not that it was a proper garden full of beautiful flowers or delicate herbs, but an overgrown monstrosity that should have been planted in the back and not near the side of the house where everyone passing by could see. That was the proper way to do things in Hamsford. But Octavia Newberry had only been a Hamsford resident for six months so she didn't know how things should be done, or worse, didn't care. She seemed the type that tended to ignore regulations and decent decorum. Why the sensible Lester Gamble had decided to rent his house to her nobody could understand. He was usually such a predictable man, but had made a very unpredictable decision to go on a year sabbatical, leaving his house to a woman no one knew anything about.

One thing that couldn't be missed was that she was very attractive. Distractingly so. Harmony had seen her own dear boy, Ray, give the hussy more than a casual glance. Twice she'd caught him helping Miss Newberry with her groceries--much more than any single woman would need-- and actually go *inside* her house instead of dutifully just leaving the items at her front door. Once he'd disappeared for so long, Harmony had visions of that woman trying devious ways to seduce him. Fortunately, she knew her Ray was sensible and old enough to know that he and that woman had little in common. Ray wouldn't be swayed by a pretty face when he should only have eyes for the sweet Amelia Dawson, an elementary school teacher. She was from a prominent Hamsford family with an excellent repu- tation. She shared Harmony's appreciation for everything beautiful. Unlike her neighbor, Amelia didn't drive a large truck and traipse around in muddy boots and jeans. As befitting her upbringing, Amelia always kept herself decent and refined, as a proper young lady should. Especially one who planned to marry an upstanding young man. When- ever she came to visit, or was in the company of Ray, Amelia was the picture of perfection. Her hair was impeccably groomed, makeup expertly applied, nails polished and her stylish figure clothed in a distinctive designer collection. That's the kind of daughter-in-law Harmony expected and the only kind she would accept. Her grandmother, who she'd visited regularly as a child while living in Antigua, had taught her the art of 'being a woman', just as her mother had shown her. And Harmony had learned well and married well as a result. Oh, if only Terrance, her dear husband who had passed away too soon, were still around to guide her son away from the luring call of this flashy, arrogant woman. Ray was a looker too. Smart, dashing and successfully running his father's business, doubling the company's profit within a year. Harmony knew he was perfect for a gold digger. But he was also very responsible and cared about his mother's feelings so she would use it to her advantage in case she needed to make him realize where his loyalty should be. This was her home and not just any woman would enter. After Terrance died, Ray had moved back home to take care of her. While she had loved Terrance, he had proved difficult at times, and hadn't managed the finances well. Ray, however, helped her maintain the lifestyle she'd always wanted.

He'd sold his luxury townhouse, moved in and upgraded their estate to all her specifications. The entire landscaping was redone, including removing several unsightly oak trees she felt dominated the front lawn. A two-level wrap-around deck, including an enclosed sunroom and greenhouse, with a fountain, had been installed in the back of the house. Harmony had a reputation and a certain standard to uphold. Ray was a considerate young man and she couldn't blame that girl for trying to catch his eye, but her son was better than some woman whose past nobody knew about. They were an established family with a reputation to maintain. The Ellis's had lived in Hamsford for generations. Her husband's great-grandfather, on his father's side, had settled there after immigrating from Grenada to Detroit, Michigan before finally moving to Maryland.

Harmony turned from the kitchen window when she heard whistling. Her heart lifted at the sound of her son's bright tune until she recognized it--it was the same tune that her neighbor was humming. "What are you doing?" she demanded when he entered the kitchen.

He paused in the doorway then flashed a wide smile use to her moods. "Good morning to you, Mother," he said giving her a kiss on the cheek.

She pushed him away. "Don't you 'Good morning' me. What are you whistling?"

He shrugged. "Just a tune I heard."

Harmony pointed to the window. "Did you learn it from her?"

He grinned. "Perhaps."

"Wipe that expression from your face. It's indecent to grin so this early in the morning."

"You're in a sour mood. Let me make you some pancakes."

"I don't want pancakes. And if I did, I would have Melva make them for me," she said referring to their housekeeper and cook.

"How about French toast?"

"No," she snapped.

"Have you taken your medication?"

"Don't change the subject."

"I didn't know we were on a particular subject."

"Ray, I don't want you near that woman."

"What woman?"

"I raised you too smart to act this stupid." Harmony gestured to the window. "She's at it again, humming like an animal in pain."

"I think she has a nice voice." Ray went over to the coffeemaker and poured himself a cup.

"Nice?" Harmony sent her son a sharp look. "She's a coarse woman moaning loudly in her garden of weeds."

He added sugar to his cup and stirred, keeping his voice neutral. "Vegetables."

"How do you know that?"

"I saw her harvesting them. She had to learn to grow vegetables out of necessity. She is from a family of eight. When she was young they had little money--"

"Then they should have stopped at two children if they had any sense."

Ray continued. "And to help stretch the family budget she grew vegetables on the little plot of land they had. There were scary times, but they were able to make it."

"So she grew up poor?" Harmony sniffed beginning to understand the tactic Miss Newberry was using to lure her son. He had a soft spot for the underdog. It was an annoying and unfortunate trait she and her husband hadn't been able to remove. They had both grown up extremely privileged and felt no shame in being so. They did their civic duties, but never felt the need to extend themselves in the way Ray did, such as giving his toys away when he was only five years old or organizing fundraisers for the local boys' group home.

"She's not poor anymore. She worked her way to--"

Harmony held up her hand. "I don't care."

"And she makes a delicious zucchini bread."

"It was edible?"

"She offered to--"

"I wouldn't accept my last breath from that woman."

"Be careful, she could be your daughter-in-law one day."

Harmony froze at the mere implication. "I wouldn't let you! Stay away from her. She sees your handsome face and deep pockets and just wants a free ride."

"No woman who kisses like her wants me just for my money."

"You've kissed her?"

More than once, but Ray was wise enough to keep that information to himself. He already found it troubling that his mother didn't like her. "Would you like coffee?" he asked eager to change the subject since he wasn't able to change his mother's mind about Octavia.

"No. How's Amelia?"

"Fine."

"She's so lovely. Sweet and considerate. You'll be taking her to Ravi's party right?"

"Maybe."

"There's no 'maybe' about it. Everyone expects you to."

Ray knew what everyone expected, but after meeting Octavia he didn't care anymore. He didn't tell his mother that he hadn't seen Amelia in months or the reason why. He'd never tell anyone what he'd overheard Amelia say to a colleague when he'd stopped by her school to surprise her last autumn.

"Of course he's going to marry me. Everybody knows it and I can tell he's thinking about asking me real soon. I expect my ring to be at least three carat. And I've got that mother of his in the palm of my hand so I'll have no problem running the Ellis estate the way I want."

Ray continued to listen as she discussed how the house would be run, where the wedding would be and the honeymoon. He debated whether he should let her know he was there or remain hidden. He decided to leave and end his relationship with her. Two days later he made it official by treating her to dinner at her favorite restaurant. He knew it was a little cruel, but he could tell by the way she was dressed and her guarded enthusiasm that she expected a proposal. Instead he calmly told her that he was broke.

She recoiled as if he'd admitted to being a criminal. "Excuse me?"

He cleared his throat and shifted in his seat, hoping to make his lie more believable by looking uneasy. "We're broke," he repeated lowering his voice as if ashamed to admit it. "The house is a money pit and business isn't as good as people think it is. My father made a number of investments that haven't worked out. I know how much you love me and want to get married, but now isn't a good time. I think we should break up."

"All the money can't be gone," Amelia said with a note of panic. "You still have the house in Barbados right?"

He shook his head.

"The flat in London?"

He shook his head again.

"But it's impossible. I can't believe this is happening to me...I mean you."

"You're the only one who knows and I'll hope you'll keep it to yourself until I figure out how to handle things." Ray cleared his throat. "I just need you to do one thing for me."

"What is it?" Amelia asked with caution, making it clear that it had better be a small favor.

"I don't want my mother to know about this. So wait six months before seeing anyone new publicly. My mother is really fond of you and I know it will hurt her if she knew we'd broken up."

"Oh sure."

"I hope we can still be friends."

"Right, of course friends," she said with a distracted air as if already trying to figure out who she would replace him with. The dinner ended soon after with both of them going their separate ways.

Ray arrived home feeling both relieved and stupid. Sure he'd been able to trick Amelia regarding his finances, but she'd conned him for even longer. He'd really cared for her and had planned his future with her plus, as she'd told her friend, his mother adored her. But she'd fooled them both by being like all the rest who only saw the Ellis fortune. He parked in the driveway briefly missing the cozy townhouse he'd decided to give up in order to keep his mother company and closed the car door with a little more force than he should have. The sweet bite of a chilly autumn wind swept past, tossing some wayward leaves in his path. He knew the leaves weren't from his trees, but their neighbor. His mother wouldn't like that. She liked her lawn pristine.

"Excuse me?" a female voice called out to him.

He turned and saw his new neighbor waving him over. He inwardly groaned. She was attractive, beautiful really, but he'd had his share of those and after Amelia's betrayal he wasn't in the mood for another pretty face or coy tactics to get his attention. If that was her intention she was going to be disappointed. Ray leaned against his car making no move to go towards her. "Yes?"

"Could I ask you something?"

He released a fierce sigh then walked over to the small hedge that separated them. "What?" he asked in bored tone.

"I need your help. I just got a delivery of mulch, but they put several stacks in the wrong location and I need to move them. I could really use your help."

Ray looked at the stack of mulch suspicious. Was this a ploy? Women had used it on him before--twisted ankles and sprained wrists--all in an effort to get his attention. He looked at his neighbor's earnest expression then back at the pile. It sounded like a reasonable request. "Okay."

"Thanks. I'll wait for you to change."

He glanced down at his clothes. She was right. He should change out of his pressed grey shirt, black trousers and dress shoes, but he wasn't in the mood. "If I go inside, I won't come back out. So I'd better help you now."

She shrugged. "Fine. Suit yourself." She turned and he followed her expecting her to point to the pile and let him do the rest, but to his surprise she picked up two bags, hefted them on her shoulders then carry them over to a far tree. He watched amazed. This was no helpless female hoping to have some big strong male come to her rescue. She was one who could handle things herself, but wasn't too proud to ask for assistance when she needed it.

Not to be outdone by her Ray picked up four bags, knowing he'd be sore the next day but not caring. He helped her move the bags and when they were finished she looked up at him and smiled. "Thanks, that would have taken me forever." She wiped her forehead with the back of her soiled glove, leaving a trail of dirt against her chestnut brown skin, then she yanked them off and held out her hand. "I'm Octavia Newberry."

"Ray Ellis," he replied liking the feel of her firm, steady handshake. He was starting to like a lot about her.

"Nice to meet you, Ray. I owe you one. Anything you want, just ask."

"I will," he said not wanting to leave. She was so beautiful yet so ordinary and it was a nice change. She didn't try to impress him with a list of degrees or family background or flaunt her figure in seductive clothes. Actually she didn't try to impress him at all. The Ellis name evidently didn't mean anything to her and his handsome face hadn't made her give him a second glance. He suddenly realized he wanted it.

Ray glanced around the yard. "Do you need help spreading the mulch?" he'd never had to do lawn work in his life--that was what a landscaping crew was for--but he'd learn if she wanted him to.

"No, but thanks for offering."

He folded his arms. He wasn't used to having a woman say 'no' to him and he didn't like it. "I'd like to call in that favor."

Octavia tilted her head to the side and grinned. "Okay, what do you want?"

"To help you with something else."

She laughed then winked, making him forget about his break up with Amelia in an instant. "When I think of something else, I'll let you know."

He rested his hands on his hips and took a step forward. "I could help you come up with some ideas."

"I'm sure you could," she said in a low, soft voice. "but not today. Goodbye." She patted his arm then turned and walked inside.

Ray didn't move. His new neighbor had suddenly become a lot more interesting. She was beautiful and strong with hips that could leave a man hypnotized.

Fortunately, it hadn't taken her long to think of something. A week later she'd asked for help with carrying her groceries, then picking vegetables from her garden, then choosing pots for her plants. Soon he was planning his schedule to make sure he was free to be with her. He was careful not to be too obvious, so their meetings were always casual and he made sure to visit Octavia when his mother was out. He knew he couldn't make his mother understand why Octavia was so special to him. Why being in her company made him feel at home, but he knew why: because she was ordinary he could be ordinary too. He didn't have to be Ray Ellis the eligible bachelor, the successful businessman, or the dutiful son. He could just be himself. Part of that unnerved him because he didn't want her to just see him as her neighbor, or worse, as only a friend. The seasons had changed from autumn to winter and now to spring, but their relationship remained friendly and casual. He wanted more.

"Octavia," he said one spring afternoon after helping her carry groceries to her kitchen. "I want--."

She covered his mouth. "Don't say it yet."

"You don't even know what I'm about to say."

"Yes, I do. I can tell by the look in your eyes. You want to kiss me right?"

*That and a lot more.* He nodded.

She removed her hand and took a step back. "Ray, there's something you should know about me first," she said in a grave tone.

His heart constricted and he felt his breathing grow shallow. He had made another mistake? Had he been duped again by a woman? "What's wrong?" he said trying to sound gentle even though he was ready to build a distance between them.

"Sit down."

He folded his arms.

"Please."

He did.

Octavia sat in front of him then told him about her past, keeping her gaze lowered her voice shaking at some points. Ray sat and listened wondering why she thought that her past would make any difference to him. He watched her wanting to gather her in his arms and let her know that none of it mattered to him, but he gripped his hands into fists instead. In an instant their relationship grew deeper not because of what she shared but because it was then that he realized how alike they were. The world outside wouldn't see it: they'd only see an attractive, at times, rough woman who'd come from a big family and risen out of poverty and a handsome, wealthy refined man who had a brother and grew up privileged. But at the core they were the same.

Octavia finally lifted her gaze. "So now you know how much I won't fit in with people like your mother--"

He stopped her words with a kiss and discovered that her lips were one of the sweetest things he'd ever tasted...

BUT RAY DIDN'T TELL his mother any of this. Instead he finished his coffee and headed off to work.

HARMONY WAS STILL in a foul mood hours later, until the latest issue of *Home and Gardens* arrived. She quickly flipped to her favorite column: *Living in Luxury*. She loved the column. She loved the advice given, and whenever she read something she wanted to add to her home, she followed it religiously. She was bothered that nowadays so many young woman didn't seem to care about beautiful things anymore. She wanted a daughter-in-law who would keep up the tradition of beautifying things, especially Hamsford Historical Gardens. The Gardens, as they were called, had put Hamsford on the map as a point of interest. Her father, a leading botanist and arborist, had been instrumental in purchasing the land and selecting the unique selection of plants and flowers from around the world that covered a total of fifteen acres. Her involvement, was limited to making special appearances but as a member of the board, she played a major role in making sure of The Gardens' upkeep.

She grew up around beautiful things; lavish flowing gardens, polished marble and oak furniture, and a wardrobe full of custom-made dresses and evening gowns. She knew the importance of proper grooming. While she understood female independence was important, she didn't want her poor boy to come home to a heated frozen dinner or take out. Or worse yet, cooking for his wife. She thought of the recently married couple she'd heard about where the husband did all the cooking and cleaning while the wife went out with her friends. Harmony shuddered at the thought. She set the magazine down and sighed. Why did that woman have to come to town? What did she do to make a living? She seemed to work odd hours. Did she have a job or was some man providing for her and she was now looking for his replacement? She was pretty enough to persuade a man to do so, but not her boy. Not Ray. No, she wouldn't worry about the lady next door. Harmony smiled and sat back down in her favorite chair and read her favorite column pushing Octavia Newberry from her mind.

Two weeks later Harmony woke up later than usual because of a cold that had kept her in bed the past week. She hated getting sick because then she was reminded of her age and it was best to forget that than remember her husband was gone and one day she'd be gone too. When that happened she feared the house would likely be neglected with no one telling Melva how to care for it. That was why it was essential that Ray married Amelia. She would know the importance of caring for the gleaming wooden railings and keeping the mantelpiece spotless. She would make sure dust never settled on the hallway chandeliers, put fresh flowers on the table in the entry way, and bake sweet potato pie or banana fritters letting the scent mingle with the fragrance of fresh lemons and ginger tea. But she wouldn't be maudlin. She was alive now and would see her son married one day to the proper woman who would become the new lady of the house, but for now she would make sure that the Ellis estate remained the darling of Hamsford's upper elite.

Every day Ray had checked in on her, fussing over her, making sure Melva cooked her her favorite green banana porridge. Her mother had always cooked it for her whenever she got sick. She pretended not to like his fussing, but was inwardly delighted by the attention. Fortunately, he seemed to take her warning about Miss Newberry seriously. Since their discussion weeks ago she hadn't seen him next door for any reason so her mood was greatly improved. Besides, today was a special day. Six months earlier she had contacted the editor of *Home and Gardens* by phone. It took several tries, a total of seven to be exact, before her insistence got her call put through. She was extremely proud to get a promise that a top speaker would come and talk to her Home Decorating Club. Wanting to make a good impression, Harmony dressed with exquisite care--making sure her hat and shoes matched and she went through her extensive collection of handbags until she found the right one. The day was perfect for their gathering. It had rained the night before, but today everything seemed fragrant and alive. Harmony left her house in high spirits, but they dipped when she saw the taxi she'd requested. She'd never learned to drive, but for a moment wished she knew how when an old rusted blue taxicab drove up to her door. She thought of calling for another cab, then checked her watch and realized she didn't have time. She'd make her complaint later. Once inside, she ignored the driver's hearty 'Good morning' and told him in clipped tones where she'd like to be taken.

Minutes later as the cab drove close to her destination, Harmony saw a glimpse of the Marquee Hotel, where the meeting was to be held, and the thought of anyone seeing her coming out of the dreadful looking thing made her heart fall. "Stop here," she told the driver.

"But we're not there yet," he said in a heavy island patois that made her wince.

"I want to get out here." She'd walk the rest of the way. She'd never let anyone see her come out of such a vehicle. She paid the driver then quickly glanced around, pleased to see no one close by--at least no one who knew her and that was all that mattered-- before exiting the vehicle. She turned as the taxi pulled away from the curb and the next moment she felt as if the sky had opened as a wave of dirty rain water came crashing down, soaking her. The taxi had driven right through a puddle ruining her outfit. She cried out to him but he was already some distance away. Her gaze darted around but there was nowhere to hide except for the parking lot. She dashed behind a car nearby and squatted wondering what to do. She pulled out her cell phone then groaned when she saw that the battery was dead. Her son was always nagging her to remember to charge her phone daily and now she wished she had listened. She'd have to find a way to get into the hotel unnoticed so she could place a call.

"Mrs. Ellis?"

Harmony briefly closed her eyes and groaned. She knew the owner of the voice before even turning--the low feminine voice stated her words like a statement rather than a question. Harmony straightened and lifted her chin, pushing the feather dripping from the front of her hat to the side. She turned and saw the last woman she'd want to see at that moment, standing in front of her wearing a cut-off T-shirt and jeans looking as if she'd come from a farm or from doing some other laborious task. Her dark hair was pulled back in a ponytail, her large brown eyes cocky and amused.

"Can I help you?" Harmony said.

A smile quirked the corner of Octavia's mouth. "I'm here to ask *you* that question."

"Do you find this amusing?"

"No, I'm sorry. That was a very careless driver."

Harmony's day was going from bad to worse. To have her clothes ruined and then have this woman see her humiliation. And--dear heavens--there was the possibility of being seen talking to her as well. It was all too much. She took a step back ready to leave. "Excuse me."

"I have a car if you'd like me to take you home."

"Listen young lady--"

"My name is--"

"I know who you are and that doesn't matter to me."

"Ray told me that today's meeting is very important to you."

Harmony gritted her teeth. It galled her that her son would share any business with this woman. It gave her a chance to gain a familiarity she didn't deserve. "I'll be fine. Excuse me." Before Octavia could reply Harmony pushed by her and raced into the hotel. The reception area hummed with people. Fortunately, she was familiar with the hotel, she'd attended many social functions there, and knew where the closest ladies' room was. She raced inside and ducked into one of the stalls. She glanced at her watch and groaned. She would miss everything.

Seconds later she heard the door open. "Mrs. Ellis?"

Harmony held her breath. Why wouldn't the blasted girl leave her alone?

"Mrs. Ellis I know you're in here."

Harmony released her breath. She couldn't just ignore

her and wish her away. "Yes?"

"Do you want me to call Ray?"

"How many times must I tell you that I'm perfectly fine. I can handle this situation without your assistance."

"You're a size sixteen, correct?"

"What?" Harmony sputtered outraged. The woman had no tact and she wore a fourteen--sometimes.

"There's a dress shop nearby. I could get you a new outfit."

"For the last time young lady--"

"My name is--"

Harmony resisted the urge to cover her ears. "I don't care. Please leave me alone and for what it's worth leave my son alone too. Am I clear?"

There was a long pause then Octavia said, "You're more stubborn than I thought."

"You haven't answered me."

"Goodbye Mrs. Ellis," she said then Harmony heard the door close.

Twenty minutes later, Harmony crept to the ladies' room door and peeked out. The reception area was clear and she had a direct line to the concierge. She took a deep breath and hurried over to him and was only a few feet away when she saw a member of her Club and darted behind a large plant. She swallowed when the woman passed by then noticed she had dropped the program. Harmony picked it up and sighed. Oh, she would miss everything. She turned the page then stopped when she saw her neighbor's name.

*We have the privileged of welcoming special guest*

*speaker Ms. Octavia Newberry. The renowned gardener and hostess has been published in Fine Living, written two best-selling books, hosted an Emmy award winning show, was a frequent guest contributor of Home and Gardens where she writes Living in Luxury with her great-aunt the renowned columnist, Margaret Whitehall. Today, Ms. Newberry will be discussing several of her gardening techniques that have revolutionized the industry.*

Harmony stared at the bio amazed. This was her neighbor? Oh what luck to have someone like that living next door! She glanced up in time to see Octavia now dressed in a fitted floral skirt and yellow gabardine blouse heading to one of the meeting rooms.

"Yoo hoo!" Harmony waved. "I see you've change."

Octavia turned and smiled. "Yes, I was just moving some garden samples for a presentation I have to attend." She turned to walk away.

Harmony took an eager step forward then stopped. "I know and I'd love to hear you speak."

Octavia glanced down at the program in Harmony's hand, quickly understanding the older woman's change of heart. "Fortunately, that won't be for another hour. I'll meet you in the ladies' room in twenty minutes."

True to her word Octavia arrived twenty minutes later carrying a clothing bag. Inside was a size sixteen baby blue sheath dress matching shoes and purse. The young lady certainly had taste. "Why didn't you tell me who you were?" Harmony asked as she admired herself in the mirror.

"You never gave me the chance."

"I'd love to have you over for dinner. I'd like you to get to know my son too."

Octavia laughed. "I'm glad to hear it because yesterday he asked me to marry him and I said yes."

# A HOME FOR ADAM

# A HOME FOR ADAM

"Send him back!"

"But he just got here."

"I know so it shouldn't be difficult to put him on a train back to where he came from."

"Claire," her husband, Jonah, said with a tired sigh. "Let's just think about this."

Claire folded her arms and shook her head, adamant. "There's nothing to think about. I don't want him here."

"But he's my sister's child."

"That sister of yours has lots of children. If she'd keep her legs closed, she wouldn't have to farm them out for other people to raise. I doubt this one even knows who his father is." She looked at the boy and shivered. "And I don't like the way he looks at me. It's as if he knows something he shouldn't."

Claire Swedan wasn't the only person to feel that way. His mother had felt the same way the moment he was born with his two front teeth intact and big brown eyes that had an eerily observant expression not seen in newborns. Adam

Trelawn was born with eyes like that of an old man: Wise, judging eyes.

Orphelia felt them watching her when she let different men into her life (especially into her bedroom) as if they were a weight of conscience that she'd ignored years ago when she'd left home to live with her first boyfriend, a man who'd said he was a musician but really made his money selling ganja (also known as marijuana), infusing the air with its smell. Adam's eyes watched in silent reproof of the cramped, dirty apartment, the always empty fridge, and the new swell of her belly that came every spring. Was it her fault that Reggie didn't like condoms or that she'd forgotten her diaphragm with Buster?

Adam quietly helped her with changing the diapers and feeding the new arrivals, but she felt his reproach and soon grew to hate him. What did a little boy know about a woman's needs? Was she supposed to be celibate because she was his mother? Was she supposed to deny herself the urges that filled her? The urge to be in a man's arms and hear him say how much he loved and wanted her—even though they were lies? She held out a faint hope that one day she would meet a man who didn't lie and she was determined not to stop until she found him.

No, Adam knew nothing about her or her needs. He was just another greedy little mouth to feed. At least Damon had money. She wouldn't let Adam make her feel guilty about that. A man with real money was a step up for her. Unfortunately, even though Adam barely spoke, those knowing eyes of his haunted her and made Damon nervous. And because there was only one male in her life who mattered to her, four days after his tenth birthday Orphelia packed Adam's things (briefly regretting that she'd no longer have free childcare) and shipped him off to her cousin, Wendy.

Wendy Lisle was a lonely woman eager for company and accepted the child who arrived on her doorstep with one suitcase and a meager two hundred dollars to cover expenses. She hustled him into her three-level townhouse and settled him in the kitchen and gave him something to eat. She imagined buying him new clothes--his trousers were too short--and getting him a nice haircut. It had been so long since she'd had someone to care for. Her husband was gone and her children lived faraway. Now she could put all her love and energy into Adam. She made him a tuna fish sandwich with thinly sliced cucumbers and romaine lettuce and set it down in front of him; imagining their new life together then she looked into his eyes and burst into tears.

She hurried out of the room and quickly wiped her eyes, surprised and embarrassed by her outburst. It must be the excitement of having someone else, she thought.

But the next day was no different or the day after that. Every time she looked into his face she was filled with a remarkable sorrow. At first she thought it was because he looked like her husband or a lost relative, but he didn't resemble anyone—it was those solemn, brown, ancient eyes. They reminded her of missed chances. She hadn't been a good wife. She'd focused on herself and couldn't make up for it now. Her husband had left her a long time ago for another woman who made him feel special and worthwhile. And her children wanted nothing to do with her. She'd been alone for a long time and welcomed her punishment. So after eight months she sent Adam packing to her Uncle Dennis: An older man who lived in a crumbly house and smelled of cigars.

At first Dennis Petrie was hesitant when he saw the boy. He liked living alone and didn't need anyone in his space. But the boy didn't seem bothered by his gruff ways. Adam had an otherworldly calm that strangely enough made Dennis angry. So angry he shattered a vase one day after watching the news and seeing the atrocities on the screen, but the boy beside him remained resolute and hopeful. What right did this child have to be calm in this awful world? A world where he'd fought in two wars and seen friends die and family members whittled away by poverty and disease. How could this child not be angered by his own unfortunate situation? Shouldn't he be at the age where he was unruly and mean? Wasn't there a reason his mother didn't want him? Instead, Adam met Dennis' rough ways with either a shy smile or a kind word. But each kind act and calm brown gaze filled the older man with anger. So he sent Adam away as well to live with his nephew, Jonah Swedan, in Hamsford, Maryland. It was a town with a large Jamaican community where old world ways sometimes clashed with modern times. Adam arrived in Hamsford taller and older (nearly twelve), but his effect on people remained undiminished.

Claire frowned. "No, I will not have him here in my house. It's bad enough we have to look after that aunt of yours, but this...absolutely not. I will not have it."

She stormed away and Jonah sighed. She was a hard woman when she made up her mind. He looked at the young boy standing in the doorway. He couldn't just send him back. He was family. He folded up the note the boy had given him and stuffed it in his pocket.

Jonah opened the door wider. "Come inside."

The boy shuffled in, but his gaze remained steadfast and Jonah understood his wife's uneasiness. There was nothing rude or arrogant about his gaze, it was just astute observation.

"Oh he's a Violet child!" a voice filled with delight said from down the hall. "What good fortune for us."

Jonah looked at his aunt and gave an indulgent smile. Her gray hair was pulled back and her fresh face beamed. She'd helped raise him and in her later years, she knew she would always have a place with him. "Sure he is."

She tugged on Jonah's sleeve. "He has to stay." She went over to the boy and reached for his bag.

Adam shook his head. "No ma'am. I can carry it myself."

She gently tapped him on the shoulder. "Don't worry, you're home now."

Jonah could tell that the boy didn't believe her and he couldn't blame him. He couldn't stay. For one or two nights maybe, but then he'd have to figure out what to do with him. "Aunty, why don't you check up on Megan?" he suggested to get her out of the way.

Before she could reply, footsteps came pounding down the stairs followed by a gasp. He turned and saw his nine-year-old daughter, Megan, and her six-year-old sister, Judy. Megan looked at her great aunt who nodded and said, "Yes, a Violet child."

Jonah lost his patience. "Aunty, there's no such thing as Violet children. That's just a story."

She shook her head. "You'll see."

Megan glanced at Adam's bag with interest. "Is he spending the night?"

"Yes."

"Great!" She took his bag before he could protest. "You can be my warrior. I was going to ask Dad, but you'll be better." She grabbed his hand. "Come on," she said then led him upstairs and Judy quickly followed.

His aunt nodded pleased. "She knows it too."

"Aunty--."

"A Violet child is a child of great wisdom. Sometimes they can uncover the deep desires of your heart, or help you heal from your lingering fears. They can even bring peace if you let them. That's something this house needs."

"This house needs new siding and flooring not another occupant."

"Don't throw this gift away."

Jonah sighed. "Our place is crowded enough and you know how Claire is when she wants something."

Her tone became firm. "You're the man of the house."

Jonah laughed. "Is there such a thing anymore?"

"Only if you choose it."

She was right. He'd let his wife rule him for years because it had been easier that way. But the child needed a home, a place to stay. He was his nephew. He could give Adam a few days and perhaps Claire would get used to the idea. But there was something strange about the boy. He was too quiet and knowing. He was the same way at dinner as he politely ate with manners Jonah knew he'd developed on his own. His sister would never have taken the time to teach a child such studious etiquette –the way he placed the napkin on his lap and ate his soup without slurping. No lifting up the bowl to get the last drop. He was so mannered and precise that Jonah almost felt like a klutz around him. Yes, he was a strange child indeed.

"I WANT HIM GONE BY MORNING," Claire said that night as they prepared for bed. She lathered moisturizer on her face.

Jonah watched his wife engage in her nightly ritual and sighed. "Why?"

"I told you why." She squirted the lotion into her palm then lathered her arms. "I don't like him. There's something wrong with him."

"The girls don't think so."

"They're children." She lathered her legs.

"Aunty doesn't think so."

Claire scowled at him. "She's an old woman."

Jonah took a deep breath. He briefly thought of closing his eyes and praying, but decided to just say what needed to be said. "I think we should give him a few days."

His wife looked at him with outrage. "What!"

"Claire, I--"

"Don't you care what I think?" She pounded her chest. "How I feel?"

It was a moment he'd been trying to avoid. Her anger always made him feel small. Guilty. "Yes, honey I do. It's just—" He heard a knock on the door and said, "Come in," glad for the reprieve. Adam stepped into the room. "Yes?"

"Can I get a glass of milk?" he asked.

Claire shook her head. "No."

"Yes," Jonah countered.

"He might wet the bed."

"He won't."

Claire walked into the bathroom and slammed the door.

Jonah turned to Adam. "I'll meet you in the kitchen," he said then went to the bathroom door ready to knock, but then he stopped and listened. He didn't hear anything breaking or the sound of her crying so that was a good sign. He would deal with her later.

He turned and grabbed his robe and left unaware that the bathroom door had opened a crack and the vicious glare of his wife followed him as he walked out the door.

JONAH WENT DOWNSTAIRS and saw the porch light on. Adam stood in the front yard looking up at the house. Jonah noticed his pajama top was too big, Uncle Dennis must have given him a hand me down. He watched the boy touch the railing then the post, looking up at a window and for a moment Jonah saw the house through new eyes. He didn't see the ugly siding or that the floors needed a new polish, but the wild wisteria clinging between the railing, the sturdy porch stairs, and the bright welcoming windows. At that moment, Adam made him feel proud of the life he'd built for himself and his family.

Adam saw him, but didn't seem startled. "I was just looking around."

"Come inside and get your milk."

Once Jonah had given him his milk, Adam took a sip then set it down and said, "I won't get to stay, will I?" It was more a statement than a question.

"I don't know." Jonah hesitated then said, "Would you like something to eat?"

Adam shook his head but Jonah didn't believe him and gave him a maroon cookie. He sent it in front of him. Adam's eyes remained lowered. He took a sip of the milk and then bit into the cookie and chewed. His face lit up.

Jonah couldn't help a smile. "You like it?"

Adam lifted his gaze. "It's the best thing I've ever had."

Those amazing, beautiful eyes hit Jonah with a pain he didn't know was possible and tears threatened to choke him. He cleared his throat and gripped his hands, desperate to control his response to the boy. He remembered being a young boy. He'd always had a home and a place to belong. Something reached deep inside him--a sense of protectiveness, a determination. This boy, this child of his blood, would never be without a home again. In his shining eyes he saw the man he wanted to be. The man he needed to be. In a moment he became the man he was meant to be: A man who would listen to his wife but not be dominated by her.

"I want to show you how to make them," he said remembering when his father had said the same words to him. He knew it was late and the boy should be in bed, but he didn't care. The boy needed good memories and he would start creating them right now. He took out the ingredients and patiently showed Adam how to make the cookies and soon the scent of melting sugar and coconuts filled the kitchen. Once they'd cooled, he let Adam take the first bite.

The boy smiled and that smile burrowed its way into Jonah's heart forever. That night Jonah tucked him in. "Sleep well, Adam. You're home now," he said.

Jonah returned to his bedroom because he knew he should, not because he wanted to. The lights were off, but he knew Claire wasn't asleep. "Adam stays."

She turned the lights on. "No."

He kept his voice low. "Yes. He stays."

Claire opened her mouth to scream, but Jonah's steady gaze forced it closed. She knew she couldn't fight him. He'd never had that expression before. He'd never opposed her and suddenly he loomed very large. He'd never appeared so tall or strong before. She wouldn't fight him tonight. She'd get rid of the bewitching boy some other way.

"Oh no!" Jonah said when he looked up from his morning paper to see a woman in a large hat walking up the drive with two women beside her. The past week with Adam had been good. He fit in easily and Jonah had prepared for a relaxing Saturday with his family, but he suddenly felt as if his luck had changed.

"What is it?" Claire said as her husband quickly removed his breakfast dishes while his children and Aunt stared at him with curiosity.

"Mother Shea is coming," he said as if their home was about to crash around them. Mother Shea was a prominent resident in their community who could make their lives either pleasant or miserable according to her mood.

Megan jumped up. "Quick Adam, we have to hide!" she said then raced out of the room with Judy scurrying behind before anyone could stop them.

"Are you sure she's coming here?" Claire asked.

Jonah folded up his paper. "Yes, I just saw her."

"What could she want with us?"

"I don't know." He glanced at his Aunty who was oddly serene, but before he could question her the doorbell rang. They both froze. When it rang again, Claire shoved him towards the door. "Go answer it while I go get some refreshments."

Jonah sighed then answered the door. Mother Shea stood with her large feathered hat blowing in the breeze her arms folded. Jonah plastered on a smile. "Mother Shea, what a nice surprise."

"We came to see him."

"Who?"

"Him."

"The Violet child," Sister Walker said when Jonah continued to look blank.

Jonah suddenly understood why his Aunt had looked so serene. "Aunty!"

His aunt hustled into the foyer looking innocent although he knew she wasn't. "Yes?"

"You've been talking."

"I only told a few people."

Jonah briefly shut his eyes and groaned.

"I think I'm catching a chill," Mother Shea said.

Claire came into the hallway and opened the door wider. "Excuse my husband, he's forgotten his manners. Please come in. There are refreshments in the living room."

The three women walked past and Jonah closed the door, giving his wife a look of surprise. "The living room? I thought you usually met in the kitchen."

"Be quiet. I want them to feel welcome."

"Why?"

"Because maybe one of them will take him off our hands."

"He doesn't need to be taken off our hands."

"But I--"

"He's staying," Jonah said then walked past her to go get Adam.

"We'll see," Claire said in a soft voice.

WHEN ADAM CAME into the living room, the three women stared at him with interest.

"He's a *meely maga* thing, isn't he?" Sister Bernice said, although she had as much fat as a paper clip. "Don't you feed him?"

"We feed him well," Aunty said.

"My *bwoy* was a lot bigger when he was his age," Sister Walker said.

"He'd still a lot bigger than most men."

"He's big boned."

"Then he must have the bones of an elephant," Aunty said.

Sister Walker bristled. "He's not handsome either."

"He'll grow into his looks."

Jonah shifted in his chair annoyed by the criticism, but knowing that was their way. "He's a good boy and causes no trouble," he said. "I'm glad he's with us."

"Who's his father?" Mother Shea asked.

"We don't know," Claire said in a low voice.

"The only father that matters is the one in heaven," Aunty said.

Mother Shea pulled a yellow scarf out of her large handbag. "Sister Swedan, I got this for you. It's expensive, but I thought of you when I bought it."

Aunty reached for it, but Adam reached forward and placed his hand on it and shook his head. "No."

Mother Shea stared at him. "What?"

"No. It's not expensive and you weren't thinking of her when you bought it."

Jonah cleared his throat. "Adam, that's not how you address an elder."

"But she's lying."

"See?" Claire snapped her fingers. "Didn't I tell you he was trouble? Mother Shea, I'm so sorry."

"Don't be," Mother Shea said taking the scarf back. "He's right."

They stared at her.

She nodded and stood. "He's definitely a Violet child. I just wanted to make sure."

With that announcement soon rumors and whispers spread through Hampsford about the Swedans' Violet child. Adam became popular throughout the community gaining a special position in the church.

Claire's annoyance grew. Wherever she went everyone spoke about Adam. She used to be a prominent person in the community, her husband a success in business, her children admired for their intelligence and good works, but now nobody cared. All that mattered was Adam, a little nobody with strange eyes and wisdom beyond his years. She tried to convince others to take him, but nothing worked. She ignored him, but no one else seemed to notice. He was popular at school, adored at home and when he came down with the flu everyone fussed over him.

Then one day Claire saw the opportunity she'd been looking for. She caught Adam taking Jonah's pocket watch from inside the curio in the dining room, and hold it in his palm. Weeks ago she'd overheard Jonah tell the boy how it had been bought by his grandfather and that he was to never touch it without his permission. As she watched the boy carefully place the item back into the curio a smile spread across her face.

When Jonah returned from work that evening, he was surprised to be met by Mother Shea, Pastor Curtis, his aunt, Claire and Adam. "What's going on?"

"I think you should sit down," Claire said.

He slowly did. "What happened? Is something wrong?"

"When the maid was cleaning the house she noticed

that your pocket watch was missing. We searched and searched and she found it in Adam's bag."

Jonah stared at Adam stunned. "Adam, can you explain this?"

"No sir."

"Did you take it?"

Claire expected him to deny it so that she could tell her story of how she'd caught him, but he looked at her and then Jonah and said, "Yes, sir."

Silence fell.

"Think about your words carefully," the pastor said.

"I have, sir."

When Jonah remained mute, Claire said, "So you're a thief. That's why your mother got rid of you."

"Yes ma'am," he said in a quiet voice.

Aunty shook her head. "He doesn't mean it."

"Why would he lie about it?"

"Come on, Adam. Tell us the truth."

"I took the pocket watch without permission," he said.

"Why didn't you just ask me?" Jonah asked feeling oddly betrayed.

"Because that's what thieves do," Claire said. "Do you see my problem, Pastor? Because he's special doesn't mean he deserves special treatment."

Jonah stood and walked over to the curio. "It could have been a mistake."

"It wasn't a mistake. He's old enough to know better."

"Be quiet," Jonah said.

Claire raised her voice. "Are you going to take his side over mine? Your wife? As he ages can we trust him? What other things will he steal? One day he could steal one of our daughters' innocence."

Jonah's eyes blazed in anger. "Never say that again. He's

my sister's child. Things like that don't happen in our family."

"They happen in every family."

"Not *every* family and especially not mine. Don't throw the shame of *your* past on this boy."

Tears formed in Claire's eyes. "Shame? You think I should be ashamed?"

Jonah sighed with regret. "No, I didn't mean it like that. But the past is over."

She pointed at Adam. "You'll let him come between us?"

"You're making this bigger than it needs to be."

"Because you're blind."

Pastor Curtis held up his hands. "Perhaps you both need a break. Old Brother Newman could use some help around the house."

"And Sister Margret could use someone to run errands for her," Mother Shea suggested.

Jonah shook his head. He didn't want his nephew used as an errand boy or a companion to an old man. He needed a home, but was his the right one? Did he have the right to ignore his wife's fears? His daughters' safety meant everything to him and Adam had disappointed him once. He thought he knew his nephew, but now didn't trust himself.

"We'll discuss this tomorrow," Jonah said.

Claire stepped towards him. "But--"

Jonah held up his hand. "Enough. Pastor Curtis, Mother Shea, thank you for coming. I'll call you with my decision." He walked them to the door.

Claire fought back a smile of triumph. She'd won. She'd put doubt in her husband's mind and within days the boy would be gone. She saw Adam sink into a chair, his gaze focused on the ground then he looked up.

Not with accusation, but knowing. A wise knowing, stripping her bare and making the expensive clothes she wore feel like rags. He knew she wanted to get rid of him and he was letting her win, turning her victory into something ugly and hollow.

"Stop looking at me," she said.

But his gaze remained steady.

She crossed the room and shook him, still his gaze didn't waver. She struck him hard across the face. His eyes filled with tears and fell down his face. One tear dropped on the back of her hand. She released him and stumbled back as the memories of her past came flooding back.

She remembered when an older cousin of hers had come to stay. He was fourteen and she was nine and everyone thought he was so wonderful while he made her life a nightmare. She remembered the different ways she tried to keep him out of her bedroom. The threats he told her if she spoke a word about anything. She remembered always feeling dirty no matter how much she bathed. She remembered the look of disgust on her mother's face when she told her, her secret.

"You're worthless and you're just jealous because everyone likes him more than you. Keep your filthy lies to yourself." She remembered how relieved she felt when he left to join the army. How she vowed that no man would make her feel afraid again—she would always rule. She would be the head. She would make the decisions. Men could never be trusted and boys were never innocent. She'd hardened herself and acquired all that she thought mattered so that no one could take advantage of her or make her feel small again.

Fortunately, sweet Jonah Swedan was perfect for her. He took her tantrums and never fought her, until now.

Because of this boy. But as she looked at Adam's tear stained face, she didn't see triumph, but cruelty. Here was innocence and she was destroying it, just as her innocence had been destroyed—with deliberate lies. How long had she let her anger against her cousin fester? How long had she let what he'd done to her rule her life until she now found herself flinging his dirty acts on a boy who'd done nothing to her?

In Adam's eyes she saw herself: The pomposity, the arrogance, the past she'd wanted to forget. This child had forced her to face the woman she'd become and the girl she had buried. It shamed her. She realized that she'd never hated him, she hated that he made all that she worshiped seem meaningless. The position at church and her reputation. Instead, he enjoyed the simplicity of life. He made everything around him become what it truly was. She fell to her knees and wept. "I'm sorry."

Jonah came into the room. "What's going on here?"

For the first time Claire saw Adam jump and saw how frightened he was. She understood his fear and knew it had to end.

She wearily stood. "I did it. I took the watch."

Jonah rested his hands on his hips and waited for her to explain.

"I wanted you to send him away, but I don't want that anymore." She swallowed then walked over to Adam. "You frightened me because...it doesn't matter anymore. Can you forgive me?"

She expected him to nod or say 'yes ma'am', but instead he hugged her then burst into tears. Claire felt the weight of his relief and sorrow. She knew he cried for her, for he was a sensitive child and knew her anguish but he also cried because of his own pain. The pain of his years of rejection of being tossed aside and discarded; years of having no place to settle, no one to claim him. Despite his gifts, he was still a boy whose mother had sent him away. She could feel that pain wash over her as his tears flowed. And she understood his need, having had a mother who was equally distant. He wanted a home with a mother and father who loved him.

Claire held him close and tight, filled with a love so great it almost scared her. As she held him she imagined holding the young girl she'd once been who desperately needed a safe place to grow and be loved. "Adam, I'll never send you away. You not only have a place in this house, but you'll always have a place in my heart."

# LOLA'S DECISION

# LOLA'S DECISION

"**L**ie!"

"I couldn't lie to them." Lola Fusamusi looked at her friend Sanya Kahn as they sat outside the campus hub of their local university. Spring seemed barely visible behind the overhead clouds, a chilly breeze blew the bare trees that had only started to bud.

On the table between them sat an empty ashtray, Sanya's half eaten veggie burger, a pile of fries and two sodas, while Sanya's overdue biology paper sat at her elbow. "The problem with you is that you're too honest," Sanya said squirting more ketchup on her fries until they were drowning. "If you don't tell your parents anything, nobody gets hurt."

Hurt. Yes, Lola wanted to avoid anyone getting hurt, but that seemed impossible. She knew her parents would be devastated if she told them she wanted to switch her major from Microbiology to Art Design. She was supposed to be a doctor and nothing else. She'd been given a plastic stethoscope at three, her own anatomy book at nine, sent off to science camp at thirteen and given a pen inscribed with 'Dr.

Lola Fusamusi' at sixteen. Her life was planned. It was not only expected, it was destined. But she wanted to fight destiny.

"You have to lie," Sanya said taking a sip of her drink. "It's not like you've never done it before. You lied for me."

Yes, many times. Sanya's parents trusted Lola and she had provided her friend an alibi for a number of dates and party escapades. To this day Mr. and Mrs. Kahn thought their second youngest had never looked at a boy, let alone kissed one. "What they don't know will make your life easier. Parents like to be kept in the dark. They want you to be their good little girl--always. Just do what Renee did."

That was too bold even for her. Renee had spent three years convincing her parents that she was going for a Nursing degree while getting one in Dance. Yes, Renee had gotten to fulfill the dream she wanted, but she had lost her parents' trust forever. People in their small community still didn't say her name. Could she risk that? Did her parents' trust matter even when it felt like a noose? If she remained the daughter they wanted her to be there would be no fights, no disappointments, and no heartbreaks. If she became the woman she needed to be, the fights and heartbreaks would come, but she would be free. Free to be herself. Lola lit up a cigarette and sighed. "I could never lie for that long."

"I thought you were quitting," Sanya said munching on a French fry.

Lola shrugged and exhaled watching the smoke dissipate. Her parents didn't even know she smoked. She hoped to quit before they found out. This time she'd lasted eight days. She looked at her friend's plate—the burger loaded with ketchup and mustard that seeped out the sides and the greasy fries. A large sugary carbonated drink sat to the side half empty. "And I thought you were on a diet."

Sanya grinned taking no offense. "It starts tomorrow."

Lola returned her grin. "Me too." *Tomorrow.* Tomorrow was always so sweet. So perfect. So full of promises. She looked forward to all her tomorrows, it was the present she struggled with.

Lola studied her friend's lovely round face. Sanya had twenty pounds to lose which she hid under dark clothes—usually black, dark blue or brown—instead of the colorful pinks, purples and yellows she wished to wear. She styled her long black hair around her face hoping it would give her face a slimming affect. Lola glanced again at her friend's plate seeing that with each fry her friend was that much further from the swimsuit she had hiding in the back of her closet. And with each puff of her cigarette Lola knew she was that much further from the healthy woman she wanted to be. Tomorrow had lied to both of them, because it was always out of reach. All they had was now. Lola absently tapped the ashes from her cigarette slowly coming to a decision. She was ready to face the consequences. Tomorrow had to start now. No more false goals. She stubbed out her cigarette. "That's the last one. I'm quitting now."

"Good luck," Sanya said with little interest.

"And I'll tell him."

Sanya paused with her burger halfway to her mouth, suspicious. "Tell him what?"

"The truth."

Sanya set her burger down and sat back amazed. "Then you're right. That is your last cigarette because your father's going to kill you."

~

Bowls of food crowded the table including the colorful reds and greens of jollof rice and a savory meat stew, the doughy consistency of *fufu* and a pitcher of lemonade. Lola let the dinner conversation pass her until her father directed a question at her. "How was school?"

She swallowed hard, gathering courage then said, "I've decided to change my major to Art Design."

"What?" her mother said.

Her younger sister Bumi stared at her dumbfounded.

Her father blinked and stared at her for a long moment then said in a calm tone, "No, you won't," before returning to his meal.

"Dad--"

He paused after skewering a mushroom with his fork. "Have I not made myself clear?"

Lola glanced at her sister, careful not to meet the accusatory glare of her mother. "I've written a few papers on art history --"

"I don't care what you do as a hobby. I am talking about your career. You don't know who you are or what you are. University won't tell you that. The Arts are for Whites, Science is for everyone. Do you think they'll welcome your work into their homes? You'll become one of the Invisible Outsiders. They only let in a few minorities. The Sciences are a more equalizing field. There's no subjectivity."

Lola bit her lip and gripped her hands at her side, trembling from rage. A rage she didn't even know she had. "I want to at least try," she said as softly as she could although she wanted to shout *Dad why don't you understand me?*

Mr. Fusamusi set his utensils down. "Try to do what? Fail? In your extracurricular activities you're free to do whatever you want. You can study Art, Philosophy, Impressionism or Literature, but your major will remain the same.

I know how seductive and romantic the Liberal Arts can be. I've studied Latin and Shakespeare. I can recite the entire text of *Treasure Island*. I am familiar with the works of Plato, Aristotle and Goethe, but a person can't live on theories. That isn't real life. There is no certainty in studying the Arts and no place for you in it. Science knows no class, no race, no limitation. It is a sound foundation."

Lola shifted in her seat, facing the cruel irony her parents had presented. The very life her parents had exposed her to they also wanted to deny her. When her mother had taken her to the opera with its Italian and French lyrics and extravagant costumes and set designs the experience entranced her, the ballet had thrilled her, the works of Charlotte Bronte and her British peers ignited her imagination. But now they were saying that wasn't her world.

Lola met her father's eyes. "Please let me try."

"You will *not* try with my money. I am paying for you to go to school to get a proper education and have a prosperous future." He shook his head and for a moment she saw his fears because they mirrored her own. "You are young and you believe that life can be fair, but the Arts offer you no certainty."

"There are few certainties in life and--"

"Says the girl who is only in her second decade," he scoffed. "What do you know about the world that you haven't read in a book? Do you think that studying great minds makes you one?"

Lola took a deep, steadying breath. "I'm not asking you to understand my desire to major in Art Design. I don't even ask that you completely accept my decision. I just want you to let me try." What she didn't say was what her heart wished. *Dad I want you to let me go. Let me be. I don't want you to feel guilty that I was born here and not back home. I know you think I have rejected my heritage, but I haven't. I carry my ancestors in my heart, in a tiny place I've slowly started to open. A place, that at times, I'm afraid to look at for fear it will be too foreign to me. Dad, father...I am still learning about myself. Let me discover who I am. No, I don't know a lot, but I do know what I want to do now.* But Lola knew better than to say this.

Mr. Fusamusi lifted his utensils and started to eat again. "You will go to sleep tonight and forget we ever had this conversation."

Lola didn't reply because what her father asked was impossible.

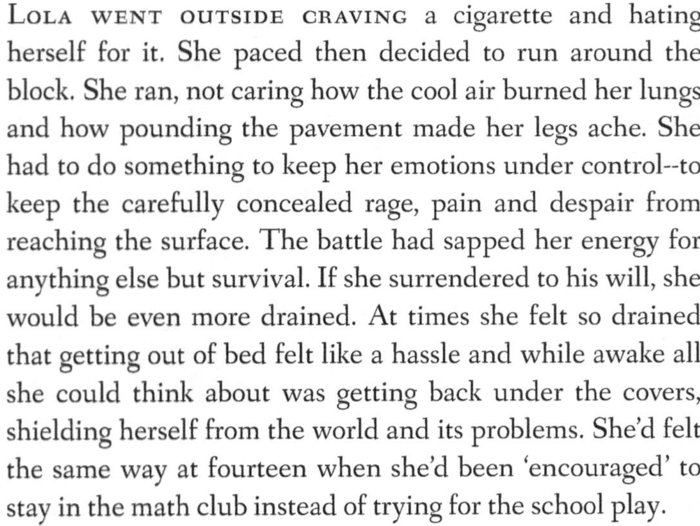

LOLA WENT OUTSIDE CRAVING a cigarette and hating herself for it. She paced then decided to run around the block. She ran, not caring how the cool air burned her lungs and how pounding the pavement made her legs ache. She had to do something to keep her emotions under control--to keep the carefully concealed rage, pain and despair from reaching the surface. The battle had sapped her energy for anything else but survival. If she surrendered to his will, she would be even more drained. At times she felt so drained that getting out of bed felt like a hassle and while awake all she could think about was getting back under the covers, shielding herself from the world and its problems. She'd felt the same way at fourteen when she'd been 'encouraged' to stay in the math club instead of trying for the school play.

As she raced past the familiar sights of her neighborhood--the pristine lawns and gardens-- she wondered how anyone managed to stay true to themselves. Or did everyone just wear a mask? She didn't really know her parents. They were just professionals who raised her. Identity didn't matter. Only duty. Lola slowed to a jog as she approached her house. She'd never had a close talk with her mother and her opinions were barely audible now so Lola no longer asked for them anymore.

She saw her mother sitting on the verandah of their suburban home. Her mother liked to sit in the wicker chair and listen to the wind chimes, humming at times or being silent. Lola remembered her saying that the chimes played a different tune each time. Lola imagined her mother anxiously waiting for the next arrangement, as if she were at a concert waiting for the orchestra to play: The wind as conductor; the chimes as the violins. Lola wasn't sure she believed the chimes played a different tune, but she'd never taken the time to listen. She was too busy. Too busy making decisions.

She walked up the steps, meeting her mother's piercing look. Her mother could always read her better than her father.

"Do you have good news for us?" she demanded.

Lola bit her lip, wondering if she should lie. "No."

"Education isn't free."

"I know."

Her mother stood. "I don't think you do." She went inside, letting the screen door close in Lola's face.

THE PHONE STARTED SHRIEKING the next day. Her grandmother from Abuja, Nigeria called to persuade her to change her mind. Her uncle living on Victoria Island in Canada called and begged her to reconsider her choice. Her aunt in London spent an hour telling her about all the trouble that could befall her for ignoring her parents' wishes. Not only had news reached abroad but the community where they lived also buzzed with the news of Fusamusi's daughter who wanted to get a useless degree. Soon the elders arrived.

"What will you do?" Mrs. Agusi said as she and two other elders of the community sat in the living room of the Fusamusi home. She was a tall woman with a booming voice as deep as a man's.

"What can we do?" Mr. Fusamusi said in a weary tone.

"Put her to work early," Dr. Alban said, his second chin quivering with indignation. He was a big man with a large appetite for food and making money. He was successful in indulging in both. "Then she will know how hard it is."

"I say marry her off," Ms. Okocha said. She was a twice divorced woman with no children, but no one held that against her because she knew how to make advantageous matrimonial matches so her advice was always requested. "I know of an excellent prospect. His family is well respected and he's ready to settle down."

Mr. Fusamusi shook his head. "It's not that simple. She's not ready to marry."

"And a woman should be able to support herself in case something happens," Mrs. Agusi added.

"Nothing will happen. The family is very wealthy and will take care of her."

Dr. Alban nodded. "You must do something before she completely shames you by wasting your money on a completely useless degree. She could end up like the Adesokan girl."

Mr. Fusamusi shuddered. The Adesokan' s forty year old daughter still lived at home after trying to be an actress and failing miserable. She ended up working in a local diner and living in her parent's basement. They didn't have the heart to tell her to go out on her own."

"Remind her of the family from which she comes," Ms. Okocha said. "The Fusamusis have been either doctors, lawyers or engineers for generations. Always. Who is she to come into this world and break that tradition? She has a great mind and so many opportunities in this country if she travels the right path."

"She knows, but she doesn't care."

The three elders released an audible gasp.

"She doesn't care?" Mrs. Agusi said. "She is that careless with her mouth?"

"She didn't say that exactly," Mr. Fusamusi corrected, ashamed he'd presented his daughter in such a bad light.

"If she won't marry or change her mind," Mrs. Agusi said. "there is only one other solution, do you agree?"

Mr. Fusamusi release a heavy sigh as he looked around the room. "Yes."

IN THE OTHER room Lola listened by the door with Bumi.

"I don't see what the big deal is," Bumi said. "it's not like you're dropping out."

Lola did. She was not just their daughter, but an extension of them. This wasn't a private family battle, but a public problem. American's celebrated individuality above all else, but not in their culture--There was 'us' not 'I'. Trying to balance the two was a constant battle. At least she knew the elders would not encourage her parents to throw her out of the house. In their community, fathers didn't do that to their daughters—sons yes, not daughters. Her friend, Titus, faced his father disowning him and kicking him out of the house when he decided to become a dentist instead of a cardiologist.

Lola thought of Titus's last email sharing his hope and pain and thought about getting a cigarette, but pushed the thought aside. She knew her disobedience would come with a punishment, but she had to be strong enough to face it.

She met her sister's worried expression with a smile. "You don't have to stay." She knew the tension in the house scared her sister; there were dark circles under her eyes. Lola kept her smile. She knew that later that evening her sister and mother would sit on the verandah and try to forget the argument that had ensued only three days ago.

"I wish I could be like you," Bumi said.

*No, you don't*, Lola wanted to say but she just playfully punched her sister in the arm. "Go away. I'm trying to listen." She turned away, letting her smile fade, wishing her sister didn't admire her. She admired her because she could still fight while most of their friends had stopped. Most of them played the game of being one thing at home and something different outside. Lola wondered if there would come a day when the impetuousness, strength and arrogance of her youth no longer motivated her or if she would simply wear a mask too. Would she one day be the one sitting in the wicker chair listening to the wind chimes, watching the leaves of the trees sway in a choreographed rhythm, casting shadows on the ground, moving like the ripples of waves down a stream, waiting and hoping for the storm in the house to pass. Too tired to move, too tired to think or try to comprehend.

Perhaps she should just give in then everything would return to normal.

"Lola. Come!"

Like a defendant standing in court to hear the jury's verdict she walked into the room and greeted the elders with an expected curtsey and then sat and waited.

"I never knew you to be a selfish girl," Dr. Alban said.

She lowered her gaze, careful to remain respectful though she wanted to argue.

"You cannot shame your father," Mrs. Agusi said. " but we've put into consideration your desires so you have two choices. Finish your degree in Microbiology or switch and lose your parent's financial support. We don't expect you to answer now. And it would be wise to think it over. That is all."

"THIS IS YOUR CHANCE," Sanya said, trying to keep up with Lola as they both raced across the campus to get to their next class. "Lie."

It had been over a week since her last cigarette and at times she felt like climbing the walls, but she was going to remain vigilant. She was already feeling healthier. "I can't."

"Haven't you learned your lesson yet?" She stopped to catch her breath.

Lola turned back to her. "What lesson?"

" Telling the truth only makes things worse. Do you really want to have to work fulltime while going to school?"

"No, but it's the only choice I have."

"No, it's not. I've got an idea."

Lola stepped closer, curious. "What?"

"Don't change your major. Let them pay for school. Once you graduate, get a job, move out and then do whatever you want. You know you can't live the way you want to and still live with them."

IT WAS A GOOD SOLUTION. Lola pondered her options as she jogged around the neighborhood. If she just followed the rules for a few more years things would be fine. Yes, she could do that. Why cause all this trouble and pain? She returned to her house and stopped in front of the window and saw her father sitting in the living room, glaring at the evening news. The room was dark, painted with the pale red of the setting sun; a signal of the coming night. The television screen reflected on the lenses of his bifocals. He didn't understand her and she doubted he ever would.

She looked behind the bushes to where she'd hidden a carton of cigarettes. She glanced at her father knowing that the news that she wouldn't change her major would bring a smile to his face. It would lift the tension in the house. She took out a cigarette then stopped and crumpled it in her fist. No, she would no longer push her feelings down with smoking or pretending to be someone she wasn't. Unlike her friend Sanya she wouldn't bury her feelings by filling her lungs with smoke or stuffing her feelings down with food, sex or drink. She wanted to be free of addictions. Especially the biggest one: The addiction to please her parents no matter what the cost.

But she also couldn't disregard their fears and hopes for her. She would try to compromise. She'd major in Art Design and minor in Microbiology that was the only balance she could think of. Satisfied, she went over to the trashcan and threw her cigarettes away then sat in one of the wicker chairs and listened to the ring of the wind chimes. For the first time in a long while she allowed a real smile to touch her mouth and felt the heavy weight of responsibility leave her shoulders. Lola jumped to her feet and opened the door ready to face her father.

THREE YEARS later Lola walked across the stage to receive her degree in Art Design. Sanya, Titus, Bumi and her mother watched her accept her degree, but the seat next to them was empty. Her father hadn't accepted her decision. She'd had to work long hours to support her education, including extending her schooling an extra year, but as she gripped the degree in her hand and left the stage she felt stronger than she'd ever felt. She knew herself. She was the woman she needed to be and she would live with pride. She hoped to make her father proud one day, but on this special day she was proud of herself and the decision she had made.

# MISS LANA WILSON

# MISS LANA WILSON

Miss Lana Wilson always did things the perfect and proper way. So when she killed herself it was no surprise that she got it right the first time, unlike sixteen year old Jeremy Howell whose rope broke, leaving him paralyzed after breaking his neck and forty year old Harry Tills who ended up a vegetable living in a nursing home. No, Miss Lana Wilson knew what she was doing. She got herself a thick, sturdy rope to carry her weight, stood on an old wooden chair and let it fall. She was found on a Saturday morning just as the sun was beginning to rise by Mr. Wallace Denton, the newspaper deliveryman she had known for years. He found her gently swinging from a wooden beam in the ceiling of her living room, for everyone to see. The drapes had deliberately not been drawn the previous night, so that she could be seen from the street. The rose colored dress she wore stood out against the background of the yellow walls like a neon sign.

SHE HAD LIVED on Beech Road all of her seventy-eight years, residing in the same two bedroom brick house she had been born in. She had seen people come and go and had lived her life quietly, writing comments to the local paper and sending letters to the editors of various magazines, which she stuck proudly on the wall. There was the letter in the late 60's to the school board to allow girls equal access to the gym as the boys; to the PTA about the importance of sex education; to the mayor when a sidewalk was put in taking up half of her front yard, and the one when she expressed her total and complete displeasure with the new traffic circle and speed bumps along Beech Road, which she felt turned her usually calm drives into carnival rides—nothing was too big or too small to escape her notice. But with the changing of the neighborhood, so it was with her letters and her impact. Her letters and opinions were rarely acknowledged anymore.

She no longer recognized the neighborhood she had grown up in. The Watsons who lived across the street, with a brood of six boys, had moved in only seven years earlier. They had destroyed much of the serenity that had existed, with their pumped up cars, which they raced up and down the street, and constant late-night parties on the weekends. Regina Musgrove and Thelma Madkin, who had been Lana's two closest friends, had moved away. One was in an assisted-living facility, the other in a senior retirement community. When she had more independence, Lana had visited her friends on a regular basis, sharing stories about catching one of her neighbor's kids trying to steal vegetables from her garden, and the youth being scared silly to find that she had rigged an elaborate alarm system that went off alerting the entire neighborhood. Or when she'd been rescued by the coast guard after the engine on her dinner cruise died. Now, she had no one with whom to share stories or her love of antiques.

She had collected an assortment of antiques, which usually looked like junk to the untrained eye, and a large collection of letters from her pen pals abroad, which overflowed out of several shoeboxes stuffed on her bookshelf. She had traveled the world without ever leaving her small town. There was Sigfrid from Sweden who she communicated with for over thirty years and Wangari from Kenya who had been her very first pen-pal. She never hated being alone, until she got sick. She was no longer able to take her bicycle rides or long leisurely walks to visit neighbors or go to the grocery store. The day before she killed herself she had sat in her favorite green armchair, which had once belonged to her father, and stared out into her garden. It was slowly being suffocated by weeds and she could do nothing about it.

"Oh my garden," she sighed. For eight years in a row her garden had won the prestigious title of Best Neighborhood Garden by the local gardening club. She'd worked hard on her garden making sure that no matter the season, there were colorful blooms on display. She especially liked the six varieties of azaleas she had planted surrounding her house. She turned to look at her antique collection of miniature figurines and posted newspaper clippings. She no longer had anyone to show them to but herself. She sighed. How she hated her illness. It made her feel weak and forced her to endure a caged existence. Never before had her house felt like such a prison. The solitude she had once regarded as a gift, now seemed a reflection of all the things she had never done – like traveling and finally meeting several of her pen pals or having her own column in the local newspaper – an offer she had received but had turned down.

She languidly stroked her fingers over the yellow and red porcelain cat that sat on the mahogany side table next to her. It dated back to the Min Dynasty, an ugly little object with its exaggerated black mouth and eyes, but it was priceless. She picked it up, bestowing upon it a mirthless smile as her eyes traced the figure with fascination. Five years ago, her house had been burglarized and the thief didn't have the sense to steal the amazing antique. He could have sold it and lived quite comfortably for the rest of his life. *People can be blind to the obvious*, she thought placing the cat back down on the table. Wasn't anyone curious that no one had seen her outside her home for weeks? Or the fact that her curtains always remained closed? Every morning, the first thing she did was open the drapes in the living room, letting the light shine in through the large bay windows. She loved to just sit and watch the color of the sky, but no longer.

The heavy footsteps of her nurse was like the sound of torpedoes dropping in on the quiet of the afternoon. She studied the woman's deadpan face (she'd seen fish show more expression) with a mixture of amusement and dismay as the nurse absently pushed aside the porcelain cat and replaced it with tea and toast--Lana's favorite snack. But, unfortunately, today the tea tasted like hot water with leaves; her toast like sawdust. Lana wondered what the woman saw when she looked at her. The nurse kept referring to her as "Sweetie" and "Honey" two terms she abhorred, and hadn't taken any time to have a conversation except to remind her when to take her pills, when to get a shower, when it was time for bed, and the end of her shift. Lana remembered the time she had cared for her own mother before she died. She made sure her mother never felt alone and that she kept her routine: Bingo on Tuesday nights at the church, the quilting bee on Fridays, and her favorite, having a pint of beer every third Saturday in the comfort of her backyard. She'd enjoyed one just two days before she passed away.

Lana's nurse took no such care. Her nurse never asked if she wanted to go for a drive or go to her favorite salon to get her hair done. But Lana took care to do her own hair, though it was becoming more of an effort. Her silver white hair was neatly braided and rolled into a bun, held in place with two jeweled hair combs she had received as a gift from a lover who's cologne she still remembered over forty years later. She knew her obituary would list her as a woman who'd never married, but she'd been loved. There had been the pilot, the senator and the architect who she'd loved, but had never admitted and lost. And strangely that's how she felt now—lost. Forgotten.

WHILE LANA SAT ALONE SIPPING her tea, in Dicken's grocery store just outside of town, Yvonne Marbles saw Fanny Daniels and eagerly rushed over to speak to her.

"I haven't seen Miss Lana Wilson come out of her house in days. Have you?"

"No," Fanny said coolly. At fifty-three she was well above the gossip of the community and didn't want to get involved with another one of Yvonne's tales. Besides, the woman annoyed her – she always had lipstick on her teeth and her cheap stockings constantly bunched up at her ankles. Fanny couldn't believe a woman of forty couldn't manage to have a neater appearance. She glanced away, hoping her cool response would dismiss her, but Yvonne continued with gusto.

"She hasn't been out of her house in a week or more and

I've seen a nurse go in," Yvonne said as she pushed her cart along. "Perhaps she's sick."

Fanny stopped and stared at Yvonne who leaned over her cart, her eyes bright with gossipy glee. "Well, then one of us should go visit her and find out."

Yvonne's attitude quickly changed. "It'll have to be you," she muttered hastily. "I'm too busy at the moment." The thought of being around a sick elderly person made Yvonne nervous. Even Yvonne's mother feared getting sick because she was certain that just a cold would encourage her daughter to immediately place her in hospice care. "I'll see you later. Call me and tell me how your visit went," Yvonne threw over her shoulder as she quickly moved to one of the checkouts.

Fanny stared thoughtfully at Yvonne's retreating form. Perhaps it was her duty to pay a visit to Miss Wilson. She hadn't in years. Fanny shook her head as she walked down the narrow aisles, blindly picking up food items and putting them in her basket. *How quick time flies*, she thought, tossing a box of crackers into her cart she'd never eat. She'd been only ten years old when she first met Miss Lana Wilson. In those days, Miss Wilson had been a local celebrity due to the publications of her tart articles in the local newspaper. Women in those days were to be quiet, but not her. She had a tongue that could cut a man in two and did so many times. A lot of people said that she ended up a spinster because no man was brave enough to marry her. No man was immune to her tongue lashings and Fanny had seen Miss Wilson in action when Miss Wilson told her father he'd better help fund Fanny's education or there would be hell to pay. And the short, balding man was no match for her when she threatened to drive business away from his corner grocery store.

Fanny got her education. She went to a nearby university, studying communications and media; she was one of only three women in her department at the time and graduated with honors. Fanny leaned heavily on her cart, remembering that victory. *I wouldn't be where I am today if it wasn't for that woman*, she thought. Miss Wilson had seen her reading a book about becoming an announcer and had encouraged her to go after her dreams, whatever they might be. For several summers, until their family moved away in her senior year, she had looked forward to visiting with Miss Wilson and sharing how well she was doing in school. Education, especially for a girl, was not a high priority in her household, so Fanny escaped whenever she could, and turned up on Miss Wilson's doorstep to have tea and cookies, before going back home. Together they'd laughed and shared secrets. The woman the town had called an 'old spinster' showing her some of the gifts men had given her over the years. But, Miss Wilson had made a vow that only one man, her father, would rule her and when he was gone there wouldn't be a replacement.

"Oh, Miss Wilson but don't you get lonely sometimes?" Fanny remembered asking her one day.

"Never. I have a full life, friends and neighbors around me. What's there to be lonely about? Besides, I like being by myself from time to time. I couldn't do that if I had a man I needed to take care of." She never said more but Fanny knew she wanted to know more. Fanny walked towards the check-out lines her head held a bit higher than usual. Yes, she decided. She would pay Miss Wilson a visit.

FANNY PACKED her groceries into her 1979 silver BMW and drove in the direction of Miss Wilson's house, which was straight down Beech Road, on the right hand side, the third house before the road ended. Fanny sped down the street, whizzing past small wooden houses, pickup trucks and jeeps that lined the road. The speed bumps and traffic circle did little to slow her. Children ran up and down the street chasing each other, while six adults glanced at them once or twice as they continued their gossiping. But they all stopped and stared as Fanny made a screeching halt in front of Miss Wilson's little brick house with its weed infested garden. The small gathering of adults and kids watched curiously as the peppered haired woman stepped out of her car and adjusted her gray silk suit and black cartwheel hat. Although she had only gone grocery shopping, Fanny had been at an official function earlier that day, and wore one of her favorite hats to match. She hadn't been on Beech Street in years and only two of the women, staring at the stylish figure, recognized her. But she was welcomed if she knew Miss Lana Wilson.

"She never married, but she's made herself a good living on the radio," a woman whispered as Fanny clicked her way up the cement driveway to the front door.

"Then she and Miss Wilson will have a lot to talk about," her friend replied. "Miss Wilson never married either."

They all laughed at the possibility that Miss Wilson even had a choice in the matter, when it came to marriage. Then their laughter died, just as quickly as it had begun as curiosity took over.

"I wonder why she's decided to visit?" another woman queried, placing her hand on her large hips as she gauged

Fanny's tailored suit and designer shoes. "She's too fancy for here."

"I guess that's why she left," a short, middle-aged woman added as she ushered her crying child up the stairs of her porch.

"I heard that Miss Wilson was sick," a little girl piped up.

"Oh. Then it's good that she'll get some company."

"Maybe I'll cook her a sweet potato pie this weekend and take it to her," her friend said. "They're in season."

"Oh and some fried chicken. She always liked my fried chicken."

The first woman piped up and soon they were all discussing what they could make for Miss Wilson before their attention shifted to the recent family drama of a neighbor and their good natured plans were soon forgotten.

FANNY RAPPED GENTLY on the red door and waited. The woman who answered it hadn't changed in over thirty years. Her 5'10" frame filled the door with her broad shoulders, thick legs and arms. She wore gray sneakers and a rose colored polyester dress she had ordered from a garden catalogue. Her wrinkled face was bare from makeup and her thin hair was pulled back into a bun. The only thing different was the cane she held off to the side.

"Why did you come?" Lana asked surprised.

Fanny only smiled and pushed past her. She made her way to the living room and immediately felt suffocated. Furniture and various trinkets filled the room and she crashed into a chair and ottoman before settling herself on the couch, which was shoved up between a large bookshelf and grandfather clock. Fanny crossed her legs, placed her purse on her lap and glanced around at the yellow walls and newspaper articles that decorated it, which had also yellowed with age. If one didn't pay close attention the articles looked like wallpaper. Fanny frowned and sat back. Years before, the posted articles had given the crowded room a sense of achievement. She remembered how eager and excited she had felt helping Miss Wilson cut out and put up some of the articles. Now they just looked tacky.

"So Miss Wilson, how are you doing?" Fanny asked, unable to rid the business-like tone in her voice.

"Why are you here, Fanny?" Lana asked again, settling in her green armchair. "You haven't come around here in a long while. Why now?"

"I met Yvonne at the grocery store and..."

"You came out of curiosity, or to see if I was dead," Lana finished. She nodded her head in a mixture of understanding and disappointment. "Well, you can see that I'm fine, so you can go now," she added, her voice carefully revealing her regret.

Fanny glanced down at her watch. "Oh, but I have some time left."

Lana was silent for a moment. "Would you like something to drink?"

"No, thank you."

Lana folded her hands in her lap and watched Fanny, her eyes sharp and assessing. Fanny was uncomfortable – she never used to be. Years ago, Fanny had welcomed herself inside the quaint house and re-read all of Lana's articles and pen pal letters in a voice she hoped to one day use on the radio, and Lana had listened and critiqued. But now the radio announcer sat silently trying to maintain a pleasant mask. *She used to be proud of me,* Lana thought.

Why is she now looking at me as though she were ashamed? Because I'm no longer young? Because I'm no longer strong? Why did she have to change just because she'd gone up in the world? I am just like her, Lana thought. But all she sees is an old, sick woman surrounded by junk, newspaper clippings and letters. Lana let her gaze scan the room and to her horror that's all she began to see too. She glanced down at her porcelain cat and slowly pushed it to the edge of the table. Then watched, with grim satisfaction, as it fell to the ground and interrupted the grating silence with a resounding crash.

Fanny leaped to her feet and pointed at the broken figure. "Oh no! Look what you did!"

Lana winced at the scolding tone in her voice. When did people think they had the right to speak to her as if she were seven years old?

"That's all right" Fanny reassured her as one would a scared pet. "Perhaps it can be glued back together."

"Perhaps." Lana sighed without interest.

Fanny gathered up the pieces and placed them on the side desk. She cleared her throat, uncomfortable with Miss Wilson's dry response. Before, Miss Wilson would have been heartbroken at breaking such an item. She looked down at her watch seeking a reason to leave.

"Did you ever see him again?" Lana asked.

Fanny froze. "What?"

"You heard me. Did you ever see him again?"

Fanny slowly sunk into her seat not sure her legs would support her. She didn't trust herself to speak.

"Fanny," Lana said in a sharp tone. "Did you ever do as you said you would?"

"Why are you asking me that?"

"Why do you think? I want to know. I read the letter

you sent him and know what you promised. Did you do as you said you would?"

"You already know the answer."

"I want to hear it from you."

Fanny shifted awkwardly, not wanting to remember Gordon Wilson, Miss Wilson's nephew. He'd been at his aunt's house almost as much as she had. He'd been bullied in and outside of school for his tall, chubby form and fascination with anything scientific. She used to listen to him talk about quantum physics as though he were reciting poetry. He, in turn, was her second greatest supporter and first love. She'd written and seen him through her first two years of college before pushing him out of her life. He was a man she still loved and whose heart she'd broken before he could break hers. She'd pushed him aside as she had Miss Wilson. "No."

"Why not?"

"I've been busy."

"People are always too busy to do the real important things. Or maybe they're just scared."

"I'm not scared."

Lana let her gaze fall and released a tired sigh. "I was. Too scared to become a columnist, too scared to say yes instead of no. I've learned that hearts heal, regrets never do."

"You have nothing to regret," Fanny said eager to change the subject. "You've lived your life just the way you wanted to."

Lana shifted her gaze to the broken antique. "Maybe." She met Fanny's gaze. "Why didn't you see him?"

Fanny shrugged trying to figure out the most appropriate lie. "By the time I thought about him again I was sure he'd forgotten about me. Like you, I didn't want any man to rule over me."

Lana sniffed. "You lied then and you're lying now. He loved you too much to hold you back. I remember the dreams you used to have before you became too educated and started to believe that you had to make a choice. He loved you and you loved him, but you lied and said you didn't. You didn't have to marry him, but you could have at least left him with the gift of your love."

"I didn't come here to talk about him," Fanny said irritated.

"I know, but I'm too old to chat about frivolous things. I don't want you to live with the same ghosts I've had. I lied to a man and have never forgiven myself. Gordon's a ghost in your life, isn't he?"

"He's married now."

"He was. Now he's a widow."

Fanny gripped her hands, hating how Miss Wilson's words made her heart race as if she were a girl of seventeen again. "Maybe tomorrow."

"If tomorrow comes. Words left unspoken, spoil."

Fanny glanced at her watch. "Hmm. I'd better go, I have to run some errands, but it's been nice to chat with you. I'll stop by again."

Lana folded her hands in her lap. "I like your hat. Promise to wear it to my funeral."

"Of...of...course," Fanny replied, alarmed by such a morbid remark.

Fanny stood eager to get away from her feeling of guilt: The guilt of never thanking or visiting one of the most influential women in her life, until now. Instead, she'd waited until they were strangers. She knew Miss Wilson could see past her tailored suit to the woman she really was. It scared her. She remembered one of the chats they had when Miss Wilson warned her not to become one of those "Snotty, upper middle-class, white collar workers who forget where they came from."

She'd listened to all of Fanny's dreams, from wanting to be an astronaut, to a chef, fire fighter and finally radio announcer. It was because of Miss Wilson's insistence that "She had what it takes" that had led her to become an announcer. She should have at least sent Miss Wilson a letter of thanks when she got her first job or to let her know about one of her many promotions. Fanny glanced at the wall again and paused when she saw that Miss Wilson had cut and posted articles about her rising career. She blinked back tears of regret. Miss Wilson had deserved more than this impulsive and awkward visit, but in a week she would visit Miss Wilson again and make it up to her.

SHE NEVER GOT THAT CHANCE. Wallace Denton found Miss Lana Wilson the next morning hanging from the ceiling and let out an animalistic scream heard by all on Beech Road. Miss Lana Wilson was buried on a Wednesday--her favorite day of the week—as specified in her last wishes. Autumn leaves fell around the mourning crowd clad in black as they hung their heads in prayer. As the coffin was lowered into the ground, Fanny watched the faces of the many individuals who had come to pay their respects. How could a woman who felt so alone have so many admirers? she wondered.

Suddenly a gust of wind blew off her hat, the very one she had worn when she had visited Miss Wilson, and set it flying through the air until it landed by a man's feet. She rushed to grab it and stumbled into him. "I'm sorry," she muttered.

"That's okay, Fanny."

Fanny stopped. She knew that voice. Her head snapped up and she stared into the brown eyes of a man who'd haunted her dreams for years. She hadn't seen him at the service because there had been so many people in the funeral chapel, but now he was all that she saw. He was no longer a chubby teenager, all that baby fat was gone, and his dark black hair was sprinkled with some gray. But one thing hadn't changed: How he made her feel. Her mouth felt dry. She didn't want to see him or have him see her, but now it was too late.

Fanny turned away and reached for her hat and again a gust of wind blew it away. It landed on top of the coffin. There was a collective gasp. At first, the crowd stared at the hat as if a unicorn had just landed, then all eyes turned to her. She thought of Miss Wilson's request to wear her pinwheel hat at her funeral and how she'd encouraged her to speak to Gordon. Evidentially she wasn't through teaching her a lesson because Miss Wilson now had her hat and Fanny was standing next to Gordon, even though she wanted to be miles away.

After a brief moment of horror, Fanny glanced at Gordon and saw his lip twitch, as if they shared a private joke, and that was all it took. She started to laugh. The crowd frowned, including the minister who had just finished the closing prayer, and sent her a disgusted glare disturbed by her inappropriate laughter.

The minister nervously cleared his throat, not used to such an unusual occurrence at such an event.

"Would you like one of us to retrieve your hat, ma'am?" he asked keeping a solemn tone.

Fanny, unable to stop laughing, only shook her head.

She covered her mouth and stumbled away, her high heels sinking into the soft grass with each step.

~

"Oh, Miss Lana Wilson," she said sobering up. "Why did you give up so soon?" Fanny leaned against a tree, wiping away tears she didn't even realize she'd shed. She watched the crowd from a distance. "We didn't see what was right in front of us." She turned and headed towards her car. "What bitter fools we are."

"Are you okay?" a familiar deep voice said. This time it didn't frighten her and she let the memories rise up—good and bad—knowing that being alive meant accepting them both.

She stopped and turned. "I am now that you're here."

A gentle smile spread on his face. "You were always to the point."

Fanny swallowed. "No, not always. I lied when I said I didn't love you." She held up her hand before he could speak, scared that she would lose her courage. "I was afraid. I've been afraid, but I'm not anymore." She took a deep, steadying breath. "Maybe one day I could treat you to coffee and we could catch up on old times?"

"I don't need to catch up on old times; I prefer talking about new ones."

"Oh," Fanny said feeling her heart pick up its pace. "Is that a yes?"

He nodded.

Fanny suddenly felt as if she were floating. "When would you like to meet?"

"How about now?"

She blinked. "Now?"

"That's what my aunt taught me. Now is all we have."

He took her hand and she let him. Miss Wilson's final lesson had been her most important one: That time was an illusion and *now* was the most precious gift of all. She thought of her hat and Gordon's hand in hers and again she laughed, brushing away a tear.

TWO STATES AWAY a letter arrived for Reginald Matthews at the Sunnytime Nursing Facility. He stared at the envelope for a long moment treasuring it because he rarely got mail anymore. When people peeked into his tidy room, they rarely saw a man who'd had a successful career as an architect designing buildings that would last generations, a man who'd traveled and had many affairs, but had never married. Most only saw a man whose hands had been crippled by rheumatoid arthritis and whose left arm was in a sling, the result of him breaking it after falling several feet after losing his grip on the staircase.

That day, no one saw the years fall away from his face as he opened the letter and stared at the handwriting, recognizing it immediately. They didn't see him smell the lavender scented paper or read the contents inside. They didn't see him re-read the letter over twenty times then turn on his CD and play songs from the 50's, remembering the dances he'd enjoyed with his first and only love. No one saw him fall asleep with a smile on his face. His nurse came in later and spotted the note lying on the bed, the smile still in place. She saw a stationary with autumn leaves and the following words:

*To my dearest love. See you soon. Forever yours, Lana.*

# A GIFT FOR PHILOMENA

# A GIFT FOR PHILOMENA

She'd never escape the kitchen--an unrelenting master that never gave her a moments rest. Philomena Hawkes wiped the sweat from her brow as the steam from the dumplings cooking on the stove filled the room. The powerful summer sun, which pressed through the window and shone on the newly polished floor, turned the small room into a domestic purgatory. The cool breath of the air conditioner couldn't abet the stifling heat from the stove and the oven, which now felt like a fiery furnace as Philly, as she was affectionately called, opened it to check her baked trout with onions and red wine sauce.

"Only three years," her older brother, Gladstone, had promised when he'd come to Jamaica to visit their parents. "Come to America and stay with me for a few years while I get my business started. You can help Helen with the household duties and then when my business is set you can go out on your own. I'll make sure that you're settled."

Philly quickly agreed to the plan and Gladstone said he'd send for her in a few weeks. Four months later her ticket arrived and Philly packed her one suitcase and dreamed of her new life in America. She knew that she and her sister-in-law, Helen, could manage the house and two children aged four and seven. However, she soon discovered that Helen had little interest in domestic duties such as cleaning the house and preparing food for her children, preferring luncheons with her friends and dinner parties instead.

"Dinners are important," she liked to tell Philly. "So that we can socialize with the right people. It's essential for Gladstone's business that he's seen in the right light." And Philly wouldn't have minded if her brother had been willing to hire a catering staff but he protested the expense. "I'm just starting out. Why don't you do it? It's only twenty people and you're such a great cook. Everyone thinks so."

So, aside from her other duties, Philly catered her brother's many dinner parties whose guest lists grew from twenty to fifty to one hundred. And as Gladstone's business grew so did his family. Although Helen was a slender woman with delicate hands and feet, she was a remarkably fertile woman and over the next eight years five children joined the household--a girl, twin boys, another boy and another girl. They were all high spirited, bright children who paid little attention to their Aunt Philly except as a domestic hand whose duty was to clean their rooms, wash and iron their clothes and fix their meals. She was the poor relation after all, a foreigner from the island who'd been given a better life thanks to their father's sacrifice.

Philly took their condescending tones and dismissive glances in good grace. Her brother and his wife didn't treat her much better so she wasn't surprised to see it reflected in their offspring.

But the three years of 'helping' slipped into ten, fifteen then twenty-five. There had been moments of envy during those intervening years as Philly saw her brother's business flourish and lovely Helen ripe with a new child. Philly ached for a home of her own: A place where she could sit in the family room and read a good book, watch a show on a large screen TV or just bask in the glow of a setting sun on a lazy autumn evening. But any moment of sitting was usually taken up with hemming an old garment, stitching a new shirt, drafting the week's dinner menu or calculating the expenses. She hadn't had a moment of quiet in years— her constant routine was going to bed late and rising early in the morning. However, Philly knew she had it better than some of her relatives. Her life here was more stable than it would have been back home. She'd received only a scant education because she wasn't bright like her brother, who'd gotten a scholarship to attend one of Jamaica's top schools, and her parents couldn't afford the fees for the one school she'd wished to attend. So from sixteen to eighteen she'd helped her father with his work but she still loved to learn. Sometimes, when her brother's family was away, she'd slip into one of the kid's room and read their textbooks amazed by the wealth of knowledge, wishing for an education of her own. That's when the question 'What could she have been?' rose in her mind and created moments of discontent.

But Philly didn't allow herself to wonder for long, she was too busy watching her brother's children grow and fulfill their destinies. There were high school graduations, college graduations, weddings and christenings. Slowly the house became empty and Philly thought her chance had finally arrived. The two youngest Hawkes children would soon leave the nest. One was a senior in high school and the other a freshman in college. But her brother bristled when Philly mentioned wanting to leave.

"With still so much to do? You won't believe the college

costs I'm paying for and I'm still paying off Anita's wedding. How can you consider leaving? At least not yet. Wait another two years. That's all I need. Aren't you happy here?"

Philly only smiled, knowing her reply wouldn't matter to him. Only cost did. She knew how much she'd saved him over the years. She saved him thousands in the cost of child care and getting a fulltime maid service like the other established families in the community. Gladstone did not like to part with his money easily and neither did his wife, who spent it freely but would never allow Philly extra pocket money to buy things.

"We'll give you whatever you need," Helen said. "Just ask." But when Philly asked for a new dress Helen offered her something she never wore or disliked from her own closet. And as the girls grew she'd give Philly their cast offs.

Philly bore her disrespect with dignity and would have been fine with an extra two years, but then Anita's marriage broke up and she moved back home with her two little girls and Philly saw her domestic duties extended for yet another generation. She could take the cleaning and the dusting, the vacuuming and the washing, but what she hated most was being stuck in the kitchen. She felt she'd spent half her life in the stifling room standing over a hot stove morning, noon and night cooking for a large family that didn't care if she'd struggled with a meat that refused to cook or a pot that kept boiling over, as long as their red beans and rice or curried goat was to their liking. Nothing but the satisfaction of their appetite ever mattered. And their careless thanks were like crumbs to a field mouse, left without regard.

Philly rested against the kitchen counter and sighed feeling old—the kitchen was her prison and the ever growing Hawkes family her captor. She pushed herself from the counter and removed the sauce from the stove, feeling a little guilty. What were a few more years anyway? She had good meals and a roof over her head. She had no marketable skills, no money of her own, or friends or relations (Gladstone was the only one of her siblings still alive—there had been two) who would want to take her in. She was completely dependent on her brother's kindness and she believed that in two more years he would let her go.

Philly glanced up and saw the mail carrier coming up the drive but gave him little notice--not knowing that he carried a package that would change her life.

~

"A package for Aunt Philly? How can that be?" Anita, the eldest, said after she'd signed for it.

Roger, the college freshman home for the summer, snatched it from his sister. "Let me see that." He shook it. "I don't hear anything rattling."

"Who'd want to send her anything? She doesn't have any friends."

Their mother, Helen, entered the foyer and took the package from him. "That might be but it's still not for you to play with." Although she schooled her features to look uninterested, she was also curious about its contents, but the name on the return label meant nothing to her. She went to the kitchen. "Philly you have something here," she said.

"Thank you," Philly said in a quiet voice. "Just set it down please."

"Aren't you going to open it?" Roger said with impatience as he watched his mother place the mysterious package on the table.

"I'll get to it later, dinner's almost ready," Philly said her voice becoming firm.

The idea of food, rather than her tone, took precedence over his curiosity and he left the kitchen to tell his siblings and father about the upcoming meal.

Anita and Helen watched Philly for a long moment surprised by her disinterest then they also left with Anita saying, "She can be such a silly old woman sometimes. She doesn't need to be so secretive. It's probably some stupid item from a catalog."

But it wasn't. Once they had all gone Philly rushed over to the package and lifted it up. She'd never received a package in her life. She looked at the name and her throat tightened as memories swept through her mind.

"So the boy wasn't lying," Gladstone said bursting into the room. "I couldn't believe it when he said you'd received something in the mail." He snatched the package from his sister. "Let me open it for you."

"I don't want to open it right now."

"I know you're busy with dinner. So finish it up and leave it to me." He pulled out a knife from a kitchen draw.

Philly gripped her hands into fists. "If you open that package, I'll burn every inch of your dinner."

Gladstone slowly looked her up and down. "You don't mean that."

Philly held out her hand. "That package is addressed to me, not you and I'll open it when I'm ready." When he lifted the knife she said, "I'll make sure your family starves tonight if you touch my box. And the next day there won't be any breakfast."

Gladstone hesitated then tossed the package at her. "No need to be dramatic. We'll be at the table," he said then shoved open the door with such force that it bagged against the wall.

Philly didn't care. She'd won a small victory against him and she'd kept what was hers.

That night—after she'd served dinner, then stacked the dishes in the dishwasher and cleaned the kitchen—Philly hurried to her room in the attic, sat on her bed and stared at the package. "Millicent Carter," she said reading the name of the addressee. She remembered that name from long ago. She'd met the young woman on her flight to America. Millicent was returning from a study abroad and the two women easily became companions on the flight. But once they reached Maryland things changed. Philly was to take a connecting flight to Illinois but planes had been grounded due to a snowstorm and she had no place to go. She was also woefully unprepared for the change in weather, her thin sweater no match for the winter chill. The clerk at the airline counter had said that the next available flight wouldn't be for another three days.

"You can stay with us," Millicent said eager to help her new friend. "You can't stay here for that long. When my brother comes to pick me up I'll tell him."

Philly shifted feeling uncomfortable. "I wouldn't want to be a bother."

"It will be fun." She looped her arms through Philly's. "We'll get to spend more time together."

"If your family agrees," Philly said cautious.

Millicent sent her a sly grin. "Once my brother sees you, he will." Philly didn't get a chance to ask her new friend about her strange statement because Millicent suddenly let out a cry of pleasure and waved. "Oh, there he is! Come on."

Millicent dragged Philly beside her and then stopped in

front of a striking looking young man wearing a dark blue cashmere coat. He was tall with haughty features and cold eyes. Philly took a step back, certain her friend was playing a trick on her. There was no possible way this cool, reserved gentleman would allow her to stay with them. Millicent didn't seem to notice her new friend's unease and offered her brother a big hug then made introductions, "Wesley this is Philomena. She's going to stay with us for the next three days."

His cold dark eyes measured her form and Philly felt her unease grow and she imagined spending the next three days in the airport terminal alone. When he shook his head her fears were confirmed. "No, this won't do," he said.

"Yes, of course," Philly agreed wanting to burst into tears, but determined not to. She had her dignity and she wouldn't shame herself, although she didn't know this country or where her next meal would come from.

"I blame Millicent for this," he said in a grave voice. "She should have known better." He took off his coat and draped it over Philly then stepped back and studied her. "That's better. We can't have you freeze."

"But you can't," Philly said stunned by his generosity.

"I can't what?"

"Give me your coat. What will you wear?"

"I'll be fine," he said then reached down and took her suitcase and one of his sister's and he and Millicent walked ahead of her. Philly quickly put her arms in the coat sleeves sinking into its warmth, the smell of honey and ginger wafting towards her and let the soft feel of cashmere touch her cheek. She'd been wrong about him; his eyes weren't cold, just serious. His face wasn't haughty but refined. Actually, he had a very nice face.

Millicent looked back at her. "Come on, Philly."

She lifted the hem of the large coat and raced after them.

Over the next three days, Millicent introduced Philly to her beloved town of Hamsford tucked on the coast of Maryland's Eastern Shore and its large immigrant population making Philly feel at home at the marketplace and little shops. Millicent immediately took Philly shopping for winter clothes and she and Wesley laughed at Philly's reaction to her first sight of snow. Philly met their ailing mother and a great aunt who lived with them. Then Millicent persuaded Wesley to make Philly his signature fudge brownies and one night he treated her to scallops and fettuccine for dinner, another night he cooked red beans and rice.

"It's his secret dream," Millicent said when Philly complimented Wesley on the meal. "He's always liked to cook."

Wesley stared at his plate clearly embarrassed by her words. "No, it's just a hobby of mine. I've never wanted to make it a profession. I have other responsibilities." And Philly soon learned what they were. During one of the quiet moments, while they strolled in the garden enjoying the crisp winter air, the smell of smoke from a distant chimney and the call of a cardinal, Wesley shared that he was struggling to keep his father's business afloat while also sending his sister to school and dealing with the health issues of his mother and great aunt.

"I don't know why I'm sharing all this with you," he said with a nervous laugh. "I'm probably boring you to tears." He smiled down at her. "But you're so easy to talk to."

"I'm happy to listen," Philly said basking in the light of his smile.

He sighed then looked at the house which needed a

new coat of paint and the roof replaced. "I want so much for my family, but after my father died…" He let his gaze fall. "I'm not sure I can make it all work."

"You will."

He looked at her, amused. "You sound certain."

"I am. You have a beautiful house," Philly said not seeing a dwelling in need of repair but a sturdy structure that had weathered many years and was much grander than the tiny two room shack she'd left behind in Jamaica. "A family that adores you and your work. Your life has a purpose. This is the land of opportunities. Seize them. I came here to help my brother, but one day I'm going to work in an office and become an executive secretary. I type very fast and I'm very detailed. I'll wear fine clothes and have a nice car and people will call me Ms. Hawkes."

Wesley laughed.

"You think it's funny?"

He shook his head. "No, I think it's wonderful. Maybe one day I'll be able to afford to hire you."

"If you ever need a secretary just ask for me, I'll come."

"Is that a promise?" Wesley asked in a low voice his expression suddenly serious, his eyes searching her face.

"Yes," Philly said, her heart beating like the wings of a mad bird trapped in a cage. She met his dark gaze amazed that she'd ever thought his eyes were cold. "Because I believe you'll succeed at whatever you try."

Too soon the three days were over. Wesley drove her to the airport and Millicent stayed behind to run some errands for her mother, but the two women hugged and exchanged addresses promising to write. Inside the airport terminal,

Philly shyly told Wesley that she hoped to hear from him too and that she knew his business would grow. He bought her a small glass figurine from an airplane shop then waited with her at the boarding gate until her flight was called.

"I won't forget you," he said in a rush before she stood in line to board the plane. "I have nothing to offer you now," he said hanging his head with regret and for the first time Philly saw how young he was—that despite his reserved nature he wasn't much older than she. "but hopefully one day I'll be able to tell you how much I—how much you mean to me." He then bent down and kissed her softly on the lips. To an outsider it looked like a quick, perfunctory kiss but to Philly it was like cinnamon butter melting on toast and far too soon he turned away. She licked her lips wanting to remember his taste and that moment forever.

"Wesley?"

He spun around and Philly rushed up to him. It was an uncharacteristic move because she wasn't usually that forward but she had to speak. "Don't forget if you ever need a secretary just call."

His face softened into a smile. "I will."

"And you can write me in-between," she said desperately wanting him too, but thinking he never would.

"I will." He nodded to the people boarding the plane. "You don't want to miss your flight."

"Yes, goodbye." She gave a quick wave.

"Goodbye."

Philly returned to the line and turned to see him one last time, but he was gone.

To her surprise and delight a letter arrived nearly two weeks later from both Wesley and his sister and they corresponded for the next three years with Philly reveling in her secret life separate from the Hawkes household. Then the letters stopped. Not returned, just stopped and bitterly Philly accepted that her new friends no longer wanted to know her. They'd grown tired of her boring life and wanted to expand to find new friends and adventures. Over the years Philly pictured Millicent getting her master's degree in social work, a goal she'd been working towards, and being promoted in the company she worked for. She saw her later marrying and having three lovely children, who were as warm and generous as she was. She imagined Wesley's business booming as her brother's had, but she didn't think of him marrying, although she knew he probably had. As the years passed she was certain they'd both forgotten about her.

But now she had this package. Her heart raced, her fingers trembled and she felt like a young girl again. She carefully opened it and saw a note:

*I hope this package reaches you. It's been a long time and you might have forgotten me but over twenty years ago we met on an airplane and spent three fabulous days together. I hope your family is well. I'm writing this note and sending this package on behalf of my brother, Wesley.*

*I know you'll have no use for a scarf in the middle of summer, but it was one of Wesley's last wishes that I send it to you (he always wanted you to stay warm) and the note attached. Call my cell phone number at the bottom if you want to talk.*

*Your friend,*
*Millicent*

Last wish? Philly thought as she took the scarf from the tissue paper that cradled it. It was a silk and cashmere mix and when she wrapped it around her neck she felt rich then she took a deep breath and read the second note scrawled in a hand she remembered only too well.

*My dear Philomena,*

*When I let you go all those years ago I never intended it to be forever. I loved you the first moment I saw you in the airport and even more as the days went by and I had every intention of asking you to marry me, to be my wife not my secretary, but I knew I wasn't in the position to ask you yet. My father's business was in a bad state and I had the obligations of my family. I couldn't bring you into my life when I couldn't provide for you. But I dreamed and planned for the day that I would be able to share not just my heart but my life with you. Fate had other plans, however. I will not bore you with the details and I am sure my silence was the best for you since you likely have a full life and family of your own. However, I hope you'll grant me the selfish pleasure of being part of your life a little longer because you were always a part of mine. Any time I was down I thought of your belief in me and it helped me to carry on. Eventually the business turned around and made a profit as did the two others I started. You deserve to share in my success so I've decided to give you my house (I hope you'll allow my sister to stay there as long as she wishes), all my investments, and I set up a trust for you so that you will be set for the rest of your life. You can retire from your job as a secretary and live life in comfort. At last I can provide for you the way I always wanted.*

*There were days that I convinced myself that you felt even a fraction of what I did for you, but after awhile I let that dream fade. Now as my life comes to an end whatever you felt for me whether as a friend or a lover, I hope you'll remember me with fondness and know that my heart was always and forever yours.*

*Wesley*

Philly's eyes filled with tears. He'd loved her all this

time and never told her. What had happened? She took off the scarf and gently placed it back in the box and let herself weep for the man she'd loved and lost. Then she wiped her eyes determined to celebrate the gifts he'd given her. With the gift of his house and money she would be free.

Free! She wouldn't have to be stuck in a kitchen. She could get out and live. Really live. She could travel and the first place she would visit would be Hamsford to see Millicent again.

~

"Travel?" Gladstone said astounded when Philly announced her plans the next day. "Where?"

"To see an old friend," Philly said.

Helen sniffed. "But who would want to see you? You don't have any friends."

Gladstone pointed at her. "And how can you afford it? Don't expect a loan from us."

"I won't need a loan," Philly replied in her usual quiet voice. "I've come into some money so I won't need your assistance any longer. I'll return and stay a week until you can find someone else."

Gladstone's face brightened. "Money? You have some money?" He clapped his hands together pleased. "That's great news! That will definitely help us."

His wife nodded. "Oh, at last I can get that new carpeting I've wanted and drapes, oh and there was this dress in the shop—"

Philly shook her head. "I have plans for the money. But we'll discuss it when I return. I'll be gone two weeks," she said then left them standing in the middle of the room, dumbfounded.

And they were even more stunned four days later when Philly emerged from her attic bedroom wearing a stylish summer dress and high heels. The Hawkes family no longer saw a dull, quiet middle-aged woman, but a beauty with smooth nutmeg skin, shining dark hair and bright brown eyes. None of them had ever noticed how attractive Philly was before. She bid them farewell then set off on her journey and as her brother watched her go, he felt as though a brightness had left their house forever. A warmth he'd taken for granted that would never be replaced.

It was just as she'd remembered, Philly thought as she stared at the old southern home. It was a little worn but fixable. She would strip the sides, replace some of the windows and add more flowers to the landscape. She walked up the driveway, stopped at the front door and took a deep, steadying breath before she knocked. Moments later a woman answered. A woman with light streaks of gray in her light brown hair and a round figure and a smile that melted away years.

"I'm so glad you're here!" Millicent said enveloping Philly in a fierce hug. When she drew back there were tears in her eyes. "Even after you called my cell phone I wasn't sure it was real. I wasn't certain you'd come and when you said in four days I couldn't believe it. Now I do."

"There are things I had to ask you in person not over the phone. The moment I got the package I had to see you again," Philly said.

Millicent's gaze fell. "Yes, the package."

Philly's joy dimmed a bit remembering the loss the package represented. "How did he die?"

Millicent turned to the door. "Come inside. It's not something to discuss on the patio and there's so much I want to tell you."

She led Philly into the family room where not much had changed. But what took Philly back was the smell of cinnamon and ginger that seemed to float from the kitchen.

"Something smells delicious. Do you need help?"

"Oh no, it's fine," Millicent said with a dismissive wave of her hand.

Philly sat, figuring that her friend probably had a cook to take care of her meals now. She crossed her legs and rested her handbag on her lap ready to get some answers. "I want you to tell me everything. What happened? Why did you stop writing?"

Millicent took a seat opposite her friend. "Our great aunt's health deteriorated to where we couldn't afford to care for her at home and had to put her into a nursing home. Soon after, she peacefully passed away, but the medical bills remained. Wesley's business continued to struggle and was close to bankruptcy. I entered a marriage I shouldn't have and soon divorced and Wesley helped with all the costs. Although he avoided bankruptcy, he didn't want to burden you with our troubles. I wanted to write you, but Wesley didn't want me to share anything with you and I didn't want to lie, so I just stopped."

"But I was your friend. I cared."

"My brother can be stubborn and proud. When the business finally turned around I drafted a letter to you eager to connect again, but then Wesley had his accident."

"Accident?"

Millicent released a heavy sigh. "Yes. He loved to go boating to relax, but a speeding boat with a group of drunken teenagers crashed into his. He was thrown overboard and his legs got caught in the propellers and were mangled up pretty bad. The surgeons were able to save his legs, but he could never use them again and he was left in a wheelchair. After the boating accident he was never the same. He became more focused on work and providing for my mother and myself, as if making up for his handicap. Mother passed away eight years ago, but he was still driven to work hard. He made a lot of money and made our lives comfortable, but he never laughed again."

Millicent hesitated. "Wesley wanted me to mail that package to you only after he'd gone. Three weeks ago he was taken to the hospital for severe pneumonia. No one thought he would recover and the doctor's weren't optimistic, so I mailed it to you." She bit her lip. "And then to everyone's amazement he got better."

Philly leaned forward. "You mean he's not dead?'

Millicent shook her head. "And I didn't tell him I mailed the package. Maybe a part of me hoped for this moment. That you'd come and give us a second chance."

Philly jumped to her feet, recognizing the creator of those sumptuous smells. "Is he in the kitchen?"

"Yes. It's his favorite place. The only place he's most like the man he used to be. We had everything designed so that he can reach things. That was the one luxury he allowed himself. He says it helps him relax. Sometimes he cooks so much we donate the extra to the local shelter and he gives lessons to single mothers and fathers who are getting back on their feet and want to know quick, cheap meals to prepare for their families. He loves it. He says it makes him feel useful."

"But I don't understand. If he's doing so well, why couldn't he have told me? He's a successful businessman, a teacher, a vibrant member of the community. I could have helped."

"He doesn't want help. And he doesn't want you to see him as he is. I think he's a wonderful viable man, but he only sees his wheelchair. The latest illness has caused some weight loss. He doesn't want you to see him as an invalid, but as the young man he was."

Philly set her handbag down. "That's too bad."

"Just be warned," Millicent called after her as Philly marched into the kitchen. "He may not be happy to see you. He's not the man you remember."

PHILLY WALKED through the kitchen door and the scents of ginger and cinnamon mingled heavily in the air along with coconut milk and fresh bread. She noticed that the kitchen was large and professional with enough ventilation to keep the room from being stifling hot. Then she saw him. His head was bent over a sauce pan. She watched him quickly stir then replace the lid before wheeling himself over to the counter and she caught a glimpse of his profile. No, he wasn't the vibrant young man he'd once been. His hair was now mostly gray, there were faint lines near his eyes, and his weight lost had aged him, but the T-shirt he wore clung to a muscled chest and arms. His back remained straight and he looked as if he'd fight any disease that tried to take him.

Philly gently knocked on the door, not wanting to startle him.

"Dinner will be ready in a minute," he said without lifting his head.

"I'm here to apply for the secretarial position. I type very fast and I'm very detailed."

Wesley spun around and stared at her.

She walked towards him. "Do you think you can use me?"

"What are you doing here?" he said in a hoarse whisper.

"Millicent sent me a package."

He ran a hand over his face and shook his head. "She wasn't supposed to send that until after--"

"You died?" Philly finished. "She told me. I'm glad she didn't wait until then."

Wesley's eyes darkened and his tone grew hard. "I don't need you to pity me."

"I don't," Philly said her tone equally hard. "I envy you."

He blinked then narrowed his eyes. "What?"

"You were successful at everything you tried. I knew you would be. Unfortunately, I wasn't. I failed. I never did train to be a secretary. I never owned a new dress or a car. No one has ever called me Ms. Hawkes with an air of respect. No, for the past twenty-five years I've looked after my brother's family burying all hopes that I'd ever have a life of my own." She folded her arms and leaned against the kitchen island. "Let me tell you what my life has been." And she did, telling him of her life of drudgery taking care of her brother's family, and the endless days and nights of labor. The hand me down clothes, the condescending looks and dark moments of lost hope. She knelt in front of him and looked up into his eyes. "Now do you see why I envy you?"

Wesley gazed down into her lovely uplifted face, humbled and ashamed that his pride and vanity had kept him away from her for so many years. He'd allowed his bitterness and selfishness to blind him from what he'd accomplished and all that he had to give. "Philomena, I'm sorry. I was a foolish man, but I wanted so much for you."

"All I've ever wanted is a home of my own where I wouldn't be berated or judged, a place where I could relax and be myself. Have I found that place?"

Wesley answered her with a kiss. Not the light kiss of youth, but the deep kiss of maturity. "You don't have to marry me to get the money," he said, taking her hand in his. "Everything is all arranged and --"

Philly shook her head. "You still don't understand. I don't want to marry you for the money. I want to marry you because you're the only man I've ever loved. That day in the airport if you'd asked me I'd have said yes."

"Even though I had nothing to offer?"

"All my life I've spent my days cooking and caring for others and just once I wanted to find someone willing to cook and care for me. That day, many years ago, I found that person in you. If you'd called, I would have come."

Wesley gathered Philly in his arms and kissed her once again, his lips reminding her of cinnamon butter melting on toast and much more. When he finally released her all bitterness, regret, and anger had left his face and only love shone through. For a moment Philly saw the young man he'd been, but quickly realized she loved the older man he'd become.

"My darling Philomena. I'll never let you go again."

Philly wiggled off his lap feeling giddy and alive. She wanted to dance and sing and laugh. But instead she walked to the pantry and grabbed an apron. "Let me help you finish dinner."

Wesley shook his head. "No. Go and tell Millicent that dinner's ready."

Philly happily replaced the apron on the hook then

pushed through the kitchen doors feeling as though she could fly. She was released from the bondage of servitude. She'd never have to cook or serve again. She had a new life and a deep love. Her American dream had finally come true.

# ABOUT THE AUTHOR

Dara Girard, an award-winning, national bestselling author of more than fifty novels and many short stories, from romance to suspense, loves telling stories.

Born in the US to immigrant ·parents, Dara enjoys pulling from her Jamaican, British, Nigerian heritage and exposure to various cultures to bring what reviewers and fans call "vivid emotional stories" to life. She is best known for her popular Henson Series, the mysterious Clifton Sisters, and the fun Black Stockings Society.

Visit her website to sign up for her newsletter and get sneak peeks, monthly updates on new releases, and special offers.

*For more information visit*
www.daragirard.com